Setting Fire to Water

Setting Fire to Water

STORIES

PHOEBE TSANG

Thistledown
Press

Thistledown Press Ltd.
P.O. Box 30105 Westview
Saskatoon, SK S7L 7M6
www.thistledownpress.com

Library and Archives Canada Cataloguing in Publication
Title: Setting fire to water / Phoebe Tsang.
Names: Tsang, Phoebe, author.
Description: Short stories.
Identifiers: Canadiana 20220153515 | ISBN 9781771872195 (softcover)
Classification: LCC PS8639.S24 S48 2022 | DDC C813/.6—dc23

Cover and book design by Grace Cheong
Printed and bound in Canada

Thistledown Press gratefully acknowledges the financial assistance of The Canada Council for the Arts, SK Arts, and the Government of Canada for its publishing program.

To my mother, Sauling Tsang,
with gratitude for the blessings of this life
and all others.

Table of Contents

A Buddhist Nativity

The Buddha has just been born. A black-haired, peach-skinned Chinese baby, plump and laughing, cradled in the arms of a white-bearded sage—Lao Tzu perhaps, or Confucius.

The setting is familiar: the atrium of a suburban shopping mall. A portable stage, legs wrapped in tinsel. A menagerie of gentle beasts, as in a Nativity tableau—lamb, horse, bull, heifer.

No reindeer. They're over at Santa's grotto.

Behind the stage, a screen-printed blow-up of a nineteenth-century Japanese landscape. Behind the backdrop, the elevators go up and down.

Saturday shoppers hurry past on the hunt for pre–Boxing Day sales. Some stop and linger, captivated by the spectacle, the way a rock near a riverbank diverts the current to a slow eddy.

A shaft of silver water falls from above the highest floor like a spotlight on centre stage.

The old man plunges the baby into the dazzling stream. The waters part. Not even one drop stains the embroidered silk swaddle.

When I was a child in England, school services and Christmas concerts made me want to believe in a Christian God. I would send silent prayers up into the vaulted darkness, the clerestory's all-seeing eyes. But the windows were closed, their stained glass colourless in the dark. My prayers never reached heaven.

The stragglers at the edge of the crowd can't see what's going on; they drift away. Those who make it to the front are amazed to discover that the animals are real. They snort, paw the stage, flick fleas from their ears, and defecate. The steam rising from a donkey's turd is redolent of jasmine and neroli.

In the Museum of Fine Arts, Boston, there is a hanging scroll: *The Death of the Historical Buddha*. Ink, colour, and gold on silk, Edo period, artist unknown. An ageless man with yellowed skin reclines on an ornate platform in a fruit-tree forest, beneath a full moon. The sage who carried him as an infant has become his grieving student, bowed and bald. Exotic animals and mythical creatures gather to pay their last respects. A dragon rends its mane. A white elephant writhes and thrashes in the dust.

The water keeps falling, like a baptism. I stand in its unstoppable flow. No past-life memory. All time is now. Wisdom is born here, straight from the source. Like those dreams where you stand naked before strangers. Now actor and audience are one. I am the baby and the ancient. I am the Buddha.

Here's a bar of soap in my hand, fragrant as chocolate. Its rich lather. I have never felt cleaner.

Hunger

1.

Light flickers across the glass-eyed houses on the other side of the highway.

Fox blinks at the glare of yellow-white headlamps roaring past, left–right, right–left. She counts: two-four-six-eight, two-four-six-eight ... The next time she gets to six, the roaring stops. Yellow dwindles to red, faraway embers. Darkness yawns.

Fox's jaws open, stretching her lips into a grin, and her tongue lolls out. Hunger wakes up in the burrow of Fox's belly, and crawls to the tip of her tongue.

Rabbit, says Hunger. Rabbit and rotten tomatoes.

Quiet, says Fox. You'll get your share.

Hunger says, You don't feed me like your mother used to.

No need to, says Fox. Not growing now.

Speak for yourself, says Hunger.

Fend for yourself.

Oh, I will, says Hunger. Just you wait and see.

The highway gleams: a hard, black river. Above this river: the sickly sweet, rotten odour of the city, wafted in from beyond the glass-eyed houses.

Here they come again: thin, shooting-star flares on the horizon, snaking down the river in pairs. Pairs of round, hard eyes, widening as they draw near.

Hunger keeps whining, but the roaring is louder.

2.

Behind Fox, farmland bleeds into meadows, bleeds into forest. Darkness spreads like a creek overflowing its banks.

There's an itch in the pad of Fox's left back paw. Must be something stuck between her toes. An ant perhaps, tangled in a whorl of matted fur. She brings her hind leg toward her nose, and nibbles between her claws. The itching stops.

Tastes good, does it? says Hunger.

Fox stops nibbling and lets her tongue hang free—the better to taste the night.

Think that'll satisfy me? says Hunger. Shut me up?

Clearly not, says Fox, bitterly.

If she can stop an itch in her paw, why not a teething stomach? How much greater the pleasure will be, when the gnawing stops.

3.

Again and again, Fox begged her mother: Tell me about when I was born.

You were the same as all my kits, said Mother. All helpless, mewling, blind.

Blind?

Your eyes stayed shut for days.

How many days?

More than eight, said Mother. Long time.

Fox tries to remember. She shuts her eyes for as long as she can, but always, Hunger interrupts. If only she could find her way back far enough and deep enough. To a darkness fuller than any night, with stars, moon, and the forest's many eyes. But no matter how fast she runs, the past is further.

4.

In the years before the highway, there were already signs of it. Years when the forest grew smaller, the wild meadows were farmed, the edge zones tidied. For years, fox parents warned that every time a kit stayed out after curfew, another tree was culled from the forest. Each time a chicken was killed but not eaten, fox parents threatened, another farmhouse would be built. When a new darkness began to snake across the greenbelt, the kits asked who the culprit was.

Shh, said their parents, the night-black river eats kits who ask too many questions. Then they tucked their noses under their tails and went to sleep.

All summer while the highway was being built, Fox watched by day from the edge of the forest and learned the smells of bitumen, gasoline, and burnt rubber. At night, when the sounds of men and machines fell silent, she inspected their work. She slipped past tapering, orange-and-white-striped boulders and crossed a smooth grey plain, soft as the half-baked, silt-clay shores of the heron pond when it hasn't rained for days. At the edge of a viscous puddle, she lowered her muzzle. An acrid aroma hissed back at her: Don't drink me.

Fox retreated, leaving a trail of paw prints, hardening.

After the last traffic cone was removed and the last gravel truck drove away, Fox padded cautiously to the edge of the verge and crouched in the tall grasses. She waited till red tail lights faded, then she crept closer to sniff the new surface. Again, that burning odour—even more pungent, but quite dead.

Suddenly, from downwind: a roar and a flash of light. Fox leapt back to the safety of the verge. Darkness could no longer be trusted.

5.

Fox learned how to count from her mother, who divided the day's spoils among her kits. In the beginning, there were eight: mother, father, and six babies. A large brood, whispered the hedgerows. Not for long, the whispers said, and soon the littlest kit was gone. One day, terror swept down out of the sky, a storm cloud with golden beak and thunderous wings. Seconds later, all that remained was a shadow growing smaller, a black spot against the sun.

After that, Mother counted her brood: two, four, six, six-and-one.

Why six-and-one? said Fox.

We have one tail, two eyes, four legs and six senses, said mother.

One nose, said Fox.

Two ears, said Mother.

How many whiskers do we have?

Count them yourself, snapped Mother.

A few weeks later, Fox saw two ears and one snout spying from the hedgerows as the kits played together in the sun. Two ears too big for a fox, one snout too long, and two yellow eyes narrowing at the smallest kit who had fallen behind. Before she started running, Fox saw one grey-brown ball of fury streaking across the meadow. Behind her, a yelp and the snapping of jaws.

Back in the den, Mother counted sadly: two, four, six.

Fox was secretly relieved. Six-and-one had been quite a mouthful.

6.

On the other side of the night-black river: tall, thin monoliths, hollow inside, with shiny glass eyes. Try as she might, Fox can't recall what used to be there, at the edge of the forest. Maybe it's because she's never been so far from home before. Maybe this world was always waiting to be discovered, with no woodland trail or animal tracks, and a river built to flow not just in two directions, but two-and-one as well—straight across.

Fox crouches up on the verge, safe in dusk shadows. Whenever there's a lull in the roaring, she raises her nose, extends her whiskers, and surveys the far shore. One by one, those glass eyes grow bright. Tiny figures move around inside, and blue lights flicker. Not like the patchwork fields dotted with ramshackle mounds of weathered brick or stone—*their* eyes are dull, cracked or boarded up entirely. Sometimes a dog, dozing outside on the end of a rusted chain. Fox always keeps her distance, just in case.

There are no dogs outside the new houses, but sometimes, from behind the twinkling eyes, Fox hears a distant yelping. And always, the roar of this man-made river. It reminds her of something she's heard before, but she can't think what. Something scared and a bit lonely, like a kit lost in the forest, crying for its mother. But not that. Not that kind of hungry.

7.

If it were up to Fox, nights would be endless. No limits to her wandering. Chasing soft, dew-drenched scents. Nuzzling each hidden fold and deepening turn of velvet darkness. Her

legs are made for running, her gait agile as her sinuous tail—
crouch, stalk, freeze, float. Her senses are attuned to speed.
The twitch of a rabbit's ear. A twig snapping underfoot on
the forest floor. The plop of a crabapple dropped from its
branch into the stream below.

When the night is over, Fox turns and retraces her tracks,
through hedges, over fences, across ditches, and under the
raised roots of an old oak tree, to rest in that welcoming
darkness called home.

Each time, she's surprised to find the den empty, save for
a small stack of dried bones. Where are Mother, Father, and
the other kits? Have they been swallowed by a darkness once
welcoming, grown suddenly vengeful? Or are they around
the next corner, just a little farther on? Somewhere back
there in the vague, shapeless past. The past being wherever
Fox has just come from, and goes back to.

There, Hunger finally grows quiet and sleeps. And Fox lies
side by side with her Hunger, as if they were lovers.

8.

For all her quickness, Fox is not a good hunter. She gives
chase, then switches targets. She catches wind of fresh game
and changes direction. She sees her prey falter, and knows
she'll outlast them. The race has already been won—why
bother finishing?

Her mother used to scold her: When will you learn?

A fox is not a fool, said Father.

What are we then? said Fox.

Clever, said Father.

Resourceful, said Mother.

We're survivors, said Father. We take what we can.

But not beggars, said Mother. We take what we need.

You mean steal, said Fox.

I have to, said Mother. I've got you lot to feed.

And me, said Hunger—but no one heard except Fox.

9.

Fox goes to the forest stream, stands beneath the apple tree, and licks its reflection. She drinks enough for six kits. Hunger splashes about in her belly, makes waves of longing. Spit pools on Fox's tongue. Her last catch was a mange-eaten mouse, slow and drunken, befuddled by poison.

You call that a meal? says Hunger.

We're different, says Fox. You like to eat; I like to run.

I am you, says Hunger. I'm all you have.

If you are me, says Fox, then two is one and one is two.

Don't be ridiculous, says Hunger. You have two ears and one tail, two eyes and one stomach.

Fox doesn't answer; it'll only encourage her.

Not that Hunger is so easily silenced. She hooks one crescent-moon claw into Fox's belly and moans into her ear: Apple pie, cinnamon bun, day-old bagel, yesterday's pizza, baked potatoes, bitter greens, baby back ribs, table scraps, poached eggs, rotten eggs, flies laying eggs, maggots on fish heads left out in the sun, garbage cans overflowing, back of the butcher's shop.

Hunger sinks her claw deeper, and tugs. Fox howls.

10.

Fox loses count of how many nights she's come home empty. The forest is smaller and more tired, the prey more scarce, the dogs fiercer, better fed. Is that roaring from beyond the forest, or the darkness within her?

The more she runs, the less she remembers. But sometimes, just before she falls asleep, she catches a whiff of it. That time her mother brought home a half-stunned vole for the kits to sharpen their claws on. Fox watched as her siblings batted the bloodied rodent from one side of the den to the other while it screamed murder.

Your mother fed us well, says Hunger.

Then find someone else to feed you, Fox says.

You always give me something in the end.

Fox laughs. I've got no choice.

You choose to live, don't you?

Fox thinks it over. She doesn't like to think, as a general rule. Thoughts move too slowly to hold her interest. But these thoughts are marching like worker ants across the floor of her den, unstoppable, heading for the bone pile.

Does Fox choose to live? Or is it just what she's always done, how she was raised, like it or not? Is this business of living the only thing that binds Hunger to Fox?

She crouches low, belly to ground, and narrows her eyes at that hypnotic, indefatigable line. One and one and one and—

Wake up! says Hunger.

Fox sits up and nips herself awake.

Look, ants! says Hunger. Crispy. Crunchy.

Fox wrinkles her nose, detects nothing but her own tired, stale scent.

Not real ants, she yawns.

What?

Can't eat those. They just look like you can.

Prove it.

All right, says Fox. But you'll have to be quiet.

Why?

You'll scare them away.

To her surprise, Hunger obeys.

Fox crouches back down, ears cocked, tail tensed. One and one and one and—better check that Hunger's still awake.

Hey there, says Fox softly. How hungry are you?

She hears a sigh, like wind rustling the bushes by the mouth of the den.

Me too, Fox whispers. Me too.

All day and all night, Fox huddles in her den. If Hunger complains, Fox doesn't hear her. Fox is transfixed by her pilgrim thoughts, an unbroken stream going both ways now, farther, closer, in and out of focus. Perhaps if she stares hard enough, she will see the crack where Hunger got in. The chink in the wall of her, where Hunger slipped through like a shard of light, piercing darkness.

11.

The next day, toward sunset, Fox can hear the rumbling in her stomach.

Let me guess, says Fox. You're hungry.

Hunger growls, Don't try to be cute with me.

I've been thinking, Fox says. She takes a deep breath. Closes her eyes for a moment and sees the ants marching in fearless procession. She says: I thought you could stay home tonight while I get us dinner.

Why? Hunger sounds cagey.

You'll slow me down, Fox says. It'll be faster with just one of me.

How much faster?

Oh, says Fox, two, four, six, maybe eight.

Eight what?

Fox thinks for a moment—she's getting quite good at this.

Eight hours, she says.

How long is that?

Like the blink of an eye, says Fox. She can't believe it's this easy to fool Hunger.

Fine, says Hunger. It's about time you took care of me.

Fox slips out of the den without a backward sniff, before Hunger can change her mind.

12.

Past the whispering oaks, after the moonlit stream where Fox paused to lap the liquid silver, and through the whispering hedgerows that call out to her:

Where are you going, four paws, two eyes and one tail? Stay away from the night-black river, or it will eat you alive. No one's faster than light.

Fox sets her nose to horizon and breaks into a trot.

She smells the highway before she can see it. Miles of black asphalt cleaving fields, searing earth.

Up on the grass verge, Fox hesitates. She doesn't normally hesitate, but that's back home in the forest. Here, her paws tremble and her tail switches left-right-left.

If Hunger were here, she'd be baying for blood.

This is where we differ, thinks Fox. Why chase what comes to you freely? The scent is enough.

But still, her nose moistens and her tail stiffens.

What lies beyond the roaring? More houses, with the same blue light behind each of their dead-fish eyes? Another river; more torrents of mouth-watering pleasure?

Between the dying of the red embers and the coming of each new wave, a long stillness. And in that stillness, nothing but the sinewy darkness of this strange river whose name is road.

Fox feels a pang in her stomach—like something Hunger would do, but sweeter. The scents of the city drift over the highway, calling to her.

Come chase us, they say.

Fox frowns. She is looking for the way in.

The scents swirl: Over here, come play.

· Quiet, says Fox, I can't hear myself think.

Here come the yellow-white flares rushing toward her from the horizon, two round, hard eyes widening, meeting Fox's unwavering gaze.

Wherever light gets in, so can she.

Fox flies down on the grassy verge, a flash of rust-red to white-tipped tail, fleeting, bright, merging with the oncoming light.

13.

Why did the fox cross the road?

She didn't.

That's not Fox lying there in the wake of vanishing tail lights. That's not her heart still pulsing, emptying itself, while a black-red pool spreads beneath her. Those aren't scavenger crows edging closer, silent for once.

While Fox's heart keeps counting—one-two ... one-two ... one-two—Fox watches from the far side of the road where she clambered as soon as the cars got too close. Now, she approaches the crumpled shape lying on the blacktop, and sniffs it.

Oh, it's you, says Fox. I told you to stay home.

Before she can blink, the headlamps are upon her. Fox sees clearly the still, sleeping body of a fox, its burnished coat shimmering with ruby flecks. We could be twins, she thinks. Then the headlamps swerve to one side and pass.

Now that she's on the other side, those new houses are bigger than they seemed, and brighter. Between the houses, every space is flooded with garish light—nowhere for darkness to hide. Above the streetlamps and neon signs: a pale grey sky with a few dim stars. Somewhere in the distance, a dog barks.

This must be what light does, once it finds a hole in the viscous dark. It slips in and replaces the past.

Soon, dawn will be here. Fox waits for the familiar longing to awaken within her, with plaintive cries and unsheathed claws.

Hurry, Fox calls softly. Let's go.

For a moment it seems the fox in the road might be stirring, then she sees it's just the wind ruffling its pelt. But what's that dark silhouette lying beside it? As the new day flickers to life, this darkness grows clearer.

Fox's heart keeps counting, quieter now. One-two … one-two …

She's so tired her paws are numb, as if she's been running for a long time. Her tongue hangs loose, but the breaths won't come. She hears the roaring, but she can't tell where it's coming from, and she can't take another step.

The last thing Fox sees is her sleek, black shadow slinking across the highway and over the verge, going back to the forest.

Imaginary Solutions

I t's the kind of café where everyone is having an affair.

A woman sits with her back to the window, both hands wrapped round an espresso cup. Her short nails are as dark as the grounds at the bottom of her cup. Each time the café door opens she glances quickly over her shoulder, then sighs with relief when it closes again.

At the bar-high window bench, a man stands before his laptop, shifting his weight from one foot to the other as if he's in a hurry to leave. He keeps looking up from his screen to the road outside, which slopes gently uphill to his right, away from the city, so that a woman walking down it may appear to float effortlessly, even in mid-August, buoyed by the lightest of breezes.

Is this why the café is chosen for secret assignations?

It can't be because of the decor. There are yellow stains on the fake marble floor, and the grouting between the tiles is black. The ceiling fans stir stale air without cooling it. The music is too quiet, forcing you to whisper.

The café owners are tired of couples who linger over single espressos while painstakingly constructing impossible questions that will never be asked. They have been married for twenty-three years and agree that all solutions are imaginary, beginning with the conception of their first child, after the husband had already met the woman who would become his mistress for the next seven years. Back then, he was still susceptible to guilt. His wife did not really believe that a baby would change him, but of all solutions it seemed the least fanciful.

His transformation from philanderer to doting father lasted for nine weeks. A month later, the wife proposed that the mistress should move in with them. The logic of this solution was so unexpected that it was hailed as a stroke of genius. To the wife, delirious from sleep deprivation, it was a matter of logistics—what with her husband MIA while she juggled child-rearing and running a café.

At first, the mistress had proved to be a wonderful babysitter. But after she gave birth to a baby boy a few years later, the wife realized her error.

"You're neglecting your own daughter for that bastard," she told her husband.

"They're both my children," he said.

"That bitch never lifts a finger around the café," she said. "Have you seen the state of the floor tiles?"

"She just had a baby," he said, weakly.

"What about when I had our Gloria? Who helped me?"

The husband knew there was no point reminding her how he'd rushed to the hospital, straight from the arms of his lover, as soon as he'd received news of the birth.

"If you dislike her so much, you shouldn't have asked her to live with us," he said. "Besides, she's in love with Frank, the mechanic."

After the mistress's departure, the husband proposed that they install a window bar, and half a dozen chrome and black leather stools to go with it.

"Why would anyone sit there," said his wife, "when we have chairs?"

The chairs were made of wicker, with red-and-white gingham cushions tied to their backs. Most of the cushions had

grown thin and unyielding with age; others had vanished
on their annual trip to the cleaners, never to be seen again.

"When was the last time you sat in one of those chairs?"
said the husband, incredulous. "Break your back, they would."

"Why would I sit in them?" said his wife. "I wasn't the one
having an affair."

When the new window bar failed to deter loitering lovers,
the husband threatened to abolish the seating entirely.

"Perhaps we should start with the bar stools," said the wife,
who knew by now that compromise, which defeats both sides,
was the only reasonable response. "No one uses them anyway."

"They're too modern," said the husband. "We should never
have bought them."

This admission stunned his wife. "You were right about
the chairs," she said shyly. "We might as well throw out those
cushions while we're at it."

After the bar stools were banished to the pantry, the wife
surveyed the half-empty café, taking care to avoid her customers' furtive glances, which she took as pleas for anonymity.
If they greeted her, she pretended not to recognize them.

"We need to attract a different kind of clientele," she said.
"Families. Entrepreneurs. Students."

"Students?" said the husband. "Are you crazy? Families
mean screaming babies, and entrepreneurs will just use our
café as free office space."

"Do you have a better solution?" she said, tight-lipped.

"Fine," he said. "Let them have their affairs. But no more
free refills."

A current of hot air wafts through the café and reaches the
counter just as the barista comes out of the pantry, where the
bar stools have been stacked in a corner although they were
not made for stacking, their legs entangled like discarded

crutches. The barista bends down to place a tray of fresh sand-wiches inside the display counter and move the stale ones to the back. As she rises, she hears the front door slam shut.

Through the café window, sparkling in late afternoon sunlight, unblemished by bird droppings because the barista cleaned it this morning, she sees a man walk away with his laptop bag slung over his shoulder, toward a woman who has entered the frame from the far right. The woman walks quickly, as if she's afraid of being late, but she doesn't seem to sweat or appear breathless. Instead, she glides gracefully down the gently sloping road. Perhaps she just got out of a taxi, stopped out of sight.

Suddenly, the barista can't picture the world beyond the window frame, though she has walked here from the station and back, six days a week, for the last seven years. In her mind's eye, an impenetrable vacuum has replaced the road to both the left and the right of the café window. At some point, the two vacuums will meet, and scientists will discover what happens when two black holes can no longer escape each other's gravity. Everything that was theory will finally become fact.

This is why black isn't a colour, thinks the barista. It strikes her that the absence of light can be felt, like any other absence.

The woman who floats down the road to her lover is wearing a straw hat, with orange-petaled flowers tucked inside the hatband. The flowers have bright yellow carpels that bleed outward from the centre, each petal becoming more fiery as it tapers. The name of these flowers begins with a g, but the rest of the word is harder to remember.

Are the flowers real?

She smiles, her face upturned and slightly tilted.

He opens his arms.

The barista looks down quickly, out of habit, even though she spends her days listening to spilled conversations. She notices the cake crumbs dropped near the outskirts of tables and crushed underfoot. Their fine, pale pigment speckles the blackened grout like constellations for cockroaches. The barista weighs going back to the pantry to fetch the broom against the possibility that it has fallen behind the bar stools again. She doesn't want to have to unstack them.

If Manuel were still here, she would say, "Manuel, can you fetch the broom please?" and he would answer, "Sí, señorita, it will be my duty and pleasure," followed by a half bow. She wonders if he spoke like that to everyone or just her. Did he mean the things he said, or was he parroting classic works of English literature—required reading from an ambitious if outdated ESL curriculum?

When Manuel worked at the café, they took their breaks together and sat smoking in the parking lot while customers lined up at the counter and rang the little brass bell with increasing fervour. He was going to be an actor and could imitate the voices of all the regular customers, including their preferences for coffee with or without foam, extra shots, or extra hot. But when he spoke in his own voice, the barista wanted to close her eyes and let his Dickensian words wash over her, more lilting and melodic than any native speaker's.

Once, after the last customer had left, they closed the cafe early. It was sunset, and the world outside the window was glazed with star-thistle honey. Manuel turned out the lights and they sat together at one of the small, round tables eating day-old pastries as if they were in Zurich or Vienna. From time to time, their knees touched briefly, like fish in an aquarium. Later, when Manuel stood up and walked around the table to kiss her goodbye on both cheeks, her nose collided with his chin. He jumped backwards and said, "I beg your pardon, my lady."

"Sorry," she said, "I thought you were going to hug me."

Manuel just smiled and looked down at the scuffed toes of his Charlie Chaplin shoes.

The next day, the café owner announced that the bar stools were going into early retirement, and he could no longer afford to hire two employees.

"Who will cover me during breaks?" said the barista.

The owner surveyed his deserted shop. "There's plenty of time between customers," he said sadly.

"And how can one person do all the chores?" the barista persisted. Each trivial and essential task—sweeping the floor, cleaning the espresso machine, making egg-salad sandwiches on white, rye, or wholewheat bread—had felt like a dance routine in a Fred Astaire movie when she shared her shift with Manuel.

"You'll manage," said the owner.

The previous night, his wife had complained of a headache. That morning, she had refused to get out of bed. When he asked her about supper, she told him to make it himself. Unfortunately, he only knew how to make two dishes— scrambled eggs and spaghetti Bolognese—and he wasn't in the mood for either.

A fly listlessly circled the last of the croissants. The café owner swatted at it.

"Could you make me a cheese and pickle sandwich to go?" he said. "After you finish cleaning the windows."

"White or brown?" said the barista.

"Do you have multigrain?"

"We're out of multigrain," said the barista, with relish.

"Never mind," said the owner. "I'll pick something up on my way home."

Since Manuel left, the barista knows: no one at this café ever meets the man or woman of her dreams. Nothing ever changes in this dim and stuffy room where each day, from a corner of the ceiling, the loudspeaker streams the same music from the same radio station—music that was out of date seven years ago. She keeps planning to hook up her old iPod to the antiquated stereo system, but what's the point? There's no one to dance with, now that Manuel's gone.

The song that was playing ends. No one notices except for the woman who sits with her back to the window, her hands wrapped round her empty espresso cup. She is the kind of person who rarely pays attention to the words of a song, but if you hum a few lines of the melody, she will tell you its name, the artist who first sang it, and the year it came out.

The café door creaks open, admitting a few garbled snatches of the city's lost voices.

The woman glances quickly over her shoulder, then back across the table at her companion. His fingers iron a crease in his paper napkin; his latte is untouched. Beneath her armpits, sweat rings dampen her white silk blouse.

He watches the light sheen of moisture growing in the thumbprint-size indentation between her collarbones. That place has a name—something scientific yet beautiful—but he has forgotten it.

She thinks: If I say nothing, perhaps he'll finally ask ...

The song ends, and a current of emotion flutters like a moth's shadow across her face. The man, who is explaining the imminent merger between his company and a rival software firm, breaks off to say, "Are you all right?"

She smiles, her face upturned and slightly tilted.

There is no explanation for his sudden urge to reach across the table and touch her sleeve, hand, or cheek before the next song begins.

The Real Macaron

Laure's mom, Brigitte, is making macarons. She holds a glass measuring cup while Laure pours in sparkling white sugar and Josie watches, holding her breath.

Every once in a while, Brigitte gives the cup a little shake so the sugar peak flattens out. When the peak grazes the red line at the one-and-three-quarters mark, Brigitte says, *Merci, mon ange*. But Laure doesn't stop pouring fast enough, so Brigitte has to tip out the excess sugar.

Josie sneaks a glance at Brigitte's face, framed by wisps of blonde hair escaping from a messy yet elegant bun. She wears a frown of concentration, not annoyance.

Later, when the frothy white mixture is almost ready, Brigitte hands Josie a teaspoon, and asks her to measure out the vanilla extract. Laure hovers at Josie's side while she carefully adds half a spoonful to the mixing bowl.

What would happen if Laure accidentally pushed Josie's arm so her hand slipped, and she spilled half the bottle of vanilla? Would Brigitte yell, curse, maybe even slap her? Or would she remain unflappable—the poised and perfect mother who makes Josie wish that she, too, were French?

The macarons must sit at room temperature for an hour before being baked. Brigitte shoos the girls out of the kitchen and promises to fetch them when the macarons are ready.

She's scared we'll breathe on them, Laure says, as the girls race upstairs to her bedroom, where they will jump up and down on the canopy bed and pelt each other with pink and white pillows, till Brigitte pokes her head round the door and asks them to stop.

Why can't we breathe on them? Josie asks, as she runs after Laure.

Laure stops abruptly halfway up the stairs, almost causing a collision, and whirls round to face her friend. She puffs up her cheeks, leans forward and exhales noisily on top of Josie's head, as if she's blowing out birthday-cake candles. Josie scrunches up her nose, shields her face with her hands, and Laure bursts into giggles. Quick as a flash, Josie rises up on tiptoes, leans forward, and blows back. Laure's long, pale hair flies up around her face like fine-spun threads of cotton candy. She shrieks and pushes her hair off her face with the back of her hand, just like her mother.

When Laure joined their school last term, Miss Mayle introduced her: Laure is from Paris. I'm sure we'll all learn a lot from her.

Laure sat unsmiling at her desk, eyes downcast. Maybe she didn't speak English.

When the lunch bell sounded, the new girl didn't join the crush of students headed for the cafeteria. Instead, she pulled a pink lunchbox out of her backpack and ate her sandwich at her desk, staring resolutely out of the window as if Josie wasn't sitting just a few desks over, on the other side of the deserted classroom. Josie opened the box of stir-fried egg noodles her mother had packed, and tried to concentrate on her homework. After school, her mother would need her to help out at the restaurant.

The next day, the pink lunchbox was replaced by a shiny steel Thermos. When Laure unscrewed the lid, a strange and delicious aroma filled the room—ratatouille, Josie later learned. She recognized the scent of tomato sauce from the Italian-style pasta her mother sometimes made as a treat, but the spices were different.

Josie looked up from her cold noodles, which suddenly seemed plain and tasteless. Before she could ask what Laure was eating, the French girl put down her spoon and began gathering up her loose, shoulder-length hair, which was in danger of falling into her food. She pulled it into a high ponytail, twisted it several times around itself, then stuck a pencil through the middle.

Josie gasped—she'd made it look so easy.

How did you do that? she blurted out.

Laure didn't look at her, but a small smile lifted the corners of her mouth. She pulled the pencil out from her bun and her loosened hair cascaded back down. Then she began the whole process again, slowly this time, glancing shyly at Josie to see if she was following.

But Josie's thick, black hair refused to stay pinned to the top of her head. Each time she tried to secure it with her pencil, it uncoiled itself like the snakes on Medusa's head in her *Treasury of Greek Mythology*.

It doesn't work, Josie said, sadly.

Laure stared at her thoughtfully, lips pursed. She was probably thinking that it was Josie's fault for having such rough, coarse hair.

You just need more pins, Laure said finally. My mom has, like, one billion. She could do your hair for you.

Her English was perfect—lightly embellished with the slightest of accents.

It turned out that Laure had already been living in Canada for two years.

The girls are building stuffed-animal forts on the plush cream carpet in Laure's room, when Brigitte knocks on the door.

I have bad news, she says apologetically.

Josie has no idea what she's talking about but Laure is out of the room in a flash, bouncing downstairs with squeals of excitement: I want to taste them!

The macarons sit on the kitchen counter: speckled, egg-shaped pebbles, some cracked.

It's because you breathed on them! Laure says accusingly.

We were too many in the kitchen, says Brigitte. That makes too much humidity.

Josie's cheeks are hot. It's her fault that the macarons are ruined, even though Brigitte's too nice to say so.

I'm sorry, Josie says.

It's not your fault, *ma puce*, says Brigitte. These things happen.

Mom always gets them wrong, says Laure. She peels one flat-bottomed nugget off the baking sheet and puts it in her mouth.

That's not fair, says Brigitte. Not always!

Josie looks from Laure to Brigitte with alarm. If she ever dared speak to her own mother like that, she'd be lectured on ingratitude and disrespecting her elders.

I'm afraid these aren't my best, Brigitte says to Josie. I'll have to throw them out.

They're still yummy, Laure says. They just look weird.

Josie picks up a splotchy, browned specimen and puts it gingerly in her mouth. It looks as chewy as a shiitake mushroom. To her surprise, her teeth easily puncture its forbidding shell, and the insides dissolve into liquid sugar. All at once, she tastes Christmas: frosted lamplight and sparkling snowflakes on her tongue.

Shyly, she looks up at Brigitte. How can she explain that she's never tasted anything so magical in her life?

Don't worry, says Brigitte, I'll make sure you get a taste of the real macaron before you go home tonight.

When Laure reaches for a third one, Brigitte says, That's enough sugar on an empty stomach.

Laure giggles and shoves it into her mouth before her mother can stop her.

Maybe next time we can try a recipe from Josie, says Brigitte. What does your mother like to bake?

Josie freezes. Is that a trick question?

Firstly, her mother hardly cooks at home. She complains constantly of being tired from working all day in the Chinese takeaway restaurant downstairs, where most of their food comes from. Secondly, when she does make desserts, they aren't anything like macarons, or the puddings in the school cafeteria. Sugar-sweetened red bean soup. Silken tofu instead of yogurt or mousse.

Cupcakes, says Josie. My mother makes cupcakes.

Does not! says Laure.

That's enough, Laure, says Brigitte. Calm down, please.

Ever since Laure visited Josie's place, she keeps asking when she can come again.

Josie hadn't exactly invited her over in the first place— Laure had insisted.

It was the first time she'd brought a friend home to the apartment above the restaurant. But her mother simply glanced up from the fish she was gutting and said, You must be Laure.

Josie's mother welcomed Laure with heaping plates of hot food. Then she ushered the girls upstairs, and went back to work. For the rest of the afternoon, she would reappear at the foot of the stairs at regular intervals and holler. Josie would run down and return with a plate of barbequed pork or shrimp satay. Not once did her mother say anything about needing help in the kitchen. Not even when Josie ventured downstairs for cold drinks from the fridge. She was about to grab some cans of orange Fanta when her mother said: Ask Laure if she wants to try the chrysanthemum tea.

Josie was pretty sure that Laure would wrinkle her nose at the retiring yet bitter taste of chrysanthemum flowers. Instead, she drained her carton of cold, slightly sweetened tea, slurped loudly through her straw, and declared that it must be so cool to live above a restaurant.

I wish my mom could make Chinese food, she added.

We don't eat like this every day, Josie said, quickly.

Dinner was usually a bowl of steamed white rice with a side of stir-fried bok choy and the restaurant's most popular dish: chicken in black bean sauce. There was always a large vat of it simmering on the stove. If Laure visited more often, she'd surely grow bored—not just of the food, but of playing in Josie's cramped bedroom with the second-hand furniture, faded wallpaper, and scuffed brown carpet.

Back in Laure's room, the forts have crumbled. War is declared, with the stuffed animals as hostages.

Let's go to your house next time, says Laure.

I don't live in a house, says Josie.

Duh, says Laure.

I like your house, says Josie. I wish I lived here.

Why? says Laure.

Josie thinks: Because your mom is cool. Because she never gets mad. Because she lets you do whatever you want.

She says: Because then we could be sisters.

Laure considers this. We don't look like sisters, she says.

Josie's heart sinks. She catches sight of herself in the heart-shaped mirror on the white dressing table, and wishes her hair was like Laure's.

The first time Josie visited Laure's house, Brigitte sat her down at this very table and told her she would turn her into a princess. With furrowed brows and the help of about thirty bobby pins, Brigitte managed to fasten Josie's hair into a ballerina bun. The bun was so heavy, Josie felt as though she were practising deportment, like the Victorian school-girls in *Little Women*. For the rest of the day, she was afraid to turn her head for fear of dislodging her 'do. She hung back while Laure raced up and down the stairs and turned cartwheels down the corridor. She woke the next morning with an aching scalp.

Josie still has the bobby pins saved in her bedside drawer, useless without Brigitte's magic hands to transform her. When Laure was over, she found the pins and tried to fix Josie's hair herself, but soon gave up.

Your hair's so strong, she said, just like you.

It's too thick, Josie mumbled, and started to tie it back.

Why don't you wear it down sometimes?

Josie shook her head. Hair was supposed to lie sleekly on top of your head and fall neatly over your shoulders. If she let her thick, unruly hair do as it pleased, it would be as bushy as a lion's mane—and she had no intention of sticking out any more than she already did.

Josie's the one who was born here and speaks perfect, Canadian English. But Laure blends in effortlessly, while Josie's always last to be picked for sports teams—her and Siddhartha, the chess whizz with the skinny legs and

perpetually runny nose. Laure's been at the school for less
than a semester, and she has more friends than Josie's made
in three years. Will Laure still want to be her friend when
she realizes how shy Josie really is?

Your mom's so cool, she says to Laure, after Brigitte has
announced that she's getting back to work in the kitchen,
this time alone please and thank you very much.

Laure rolls her eyes. She's only nice when you're here.

Really? Josie tries to imagine Brigitte losing her temper.
Brigitte's soft, musical voice turning stern and staccato like
her own mother's.

Anyway, says Laure, I'm sick of macarons.

You're just used to them, says Josie. I bet the first time you
ate one, it was amazing.

I can't remember, Laure says, and yawns. I'm bored. Let's
do something else.

We could do homework, Josie says.

Yes! You can help me with math.

Josie hesitates. The other day, when Miss Mayle praised her
for getting top marks, she caught Eleanor Fairbanks whispering something to Laure.

Nah, says Josie. It's boring.

But you like math.

Josie shrugs.

Are you saying that because some of the other girls aren't
good at it?

Maybe.

Who cares what they think?

You're right, says Josie. I don't care.

Laure says: That's why you're so cool.

It's late when Josie gets home—after six o'clock. Her mother's in the kitchen, deep-frying a fresh batch of spring rolls.

Where have you been? she says without looking up.

Josie holds out a paper bag full of fresh macarons: Laure's mom made these for you.

Her mother glances inside the bag, and her eyes crease into a smile.

Macarons! she says. Real, French macarons.

You've tried them before? Josie says, incredulous.

I had them in Paris, says her mother, at a café near the Seine. It was a hot day. I remember how they melted in my mouth.

You've been to Paris?

Just for a holiday, when I was young. Before I came to Canada. I wasn't always a boring old woman, you know.

Josie imagines Paris: the smell of sugar and vanilla, and the sound of horses' hooves ringing through cobblestone streets. Beneath the twinkling half-light of crystal chandeliers, dancers twirl slowly in pastel ball gowns. Their skirts fan out like the petals of the pink-and-white hibiscus in its earthenware pot by the kitchen window that Josie has seen bloom only once, no matter how her mother prunes, feeds, and coaxes it. Among the ladies' chignons, her mother's head of boy-cut hair gleams, a pearly black.

Did you always have short hair? she asks.

My hair was longer than yours, says her mother. Maybe I'll grow it again—what do you think?

Josie stares. For as long as she remembers, her mother's hair has been cropped close to her head, except for face-framing bangs which she tucks under a visor while cooking. She tries to picture her mother with an elegant updo but it looks wrong—fussy and impractical amidst the bustle of the kitchen, the smell of hot oil and frying fat. She hears the clatter of the wok as her mother expertly turns it on the blue-flamed stove, then the rumbling of her empty stomach.

Josie giggles, light-headed.

What's so funny? her mother asks.

I don't want you to change.

What are you talking about? says her mother. Time for dinner.

She slides a plate of chicken and vegetables across the stainless-steel counter. Josie fills her bowl at the rice cooker. She can hardly wait to pull up her stool and start shovelling the fragrant, steaming rice into her mouth with bamboo chopsticks.

You were hungry, says her mother. What did you eat today?

Nothing, Josie lies.

Her mother shakes her head, and sighs wryly.

Sugar no good on an empty stomach, she says. You need real food.

Josie nods, her mouth full of garlicky chicken and salty, fermented beans. She's had this dish hundreds of times— almost every night, for as long as she can remember.

It's the most delicious meal she has ever eaten.

System Down

T he day Freeman gets arrested for being a "track-level trespasser," somewhere between the Spadina and St. George subway stations, he's on his way downtown to get his health card. Lanie's been at him for weeks about renewing it. What if he has an accident and has to go to emergency? She sure as hell isn't paying for his blood transfusion on top of everything else.

By the time the cops are done with him, it's too late to get the health card. Freeman walks home in the waning dusk because, after being questioned by transit officers and the police for two hours in a cramped underground office, he feels like an escaped lab rat.

The walk cools him off somewhat. But as soon as he sees the back of Lanie's tensed shoulders in front of the TV, his peace of mind, already fragile, evaporates.

Why? Lanie says. Why, Manny, why?

Why what?

Freeman bypasses the living room door and goes into the kitchen for a cold beer. From down the corridor, he hears the news anchor talking oil prices and the upcoming basketball game.

Do you think I'm stupid? Lanie calls, above the newscaster's voice.

Of course he doesn't think that. Why would he think that? It's not his place to question Lanie's intelligence. But how on earth could she possibly know about what happened down there, in the murky depths of the Toronto transit system, unless she has X-ray vision?

How did I know? Lanie says.

That's how Freeman realizes he's been thinking out loud.

I saw you with my own two eyes. Right here on this screen. I saw them drag you out of that tunnel.

They didn't *drag* me, Freeman says, defensively. I didn't need no help.

So it *was* you, she says. I thought I recognized your red backpack and that ridiculous beanie. I just didn't want to believe you could be so stupid.

Hey now, says Freeman. He walked right into that one, and now there's no point trying to cover his tracks.

You could have left the station and walked, says Lanie. Her voice has risen in pitch, as well as volume.

Freeman takes a slug of cold Coors Light, and heaves a gaseous sigh.

I did walk, he says, that's what I did.

You walked on the subway tracks. Who does that?

Against his better judgement, Freeman leaves the safety of the kitchen and wanders back toward the living room. He leans against the door frame and presses the cold can to his forehead.

Look, he says to the back of Lanie's head, I waited twenty-five minutes for the freaking train. You wanted me to get my health card, didn't you?

They had to shut the power off, says Lanie. They said the entire subway system was down.

Was it really? says Freeman, with an awe he can't keep out of his voice.

Until now, he hasn't had a moment to contemplate the magnitude of his transgression. Majestic waveforms of consequence rippling forth from one small act of defiance, toward the outer limits of the dizzying galaxy, diverting the magnetic fields of unborn stars.

What if his actions had gone unnoticed, and the alarm not sounded? What if he'd wandered undetected into the middle of that lightless tunnel? What if he'd tripped and fallen on the tracks?

He'd walked to the end of the platform, in front of the yellow danger sign. He vaulted the safety barrier, then lowered himself carefully onto the tracks. Once inside the tunnel, the smooth concrete floor beneath the raised rails soon gave way to rough gravel, interrupted by dirt-covered sleepers. Maintaining his footing while avoiding the live rail was harder than he'd expected. He'd been somewhat relieved when security apprehended him.

Lanie's sitting in the middle of the spongy three-part sofa, so Freeman sits down on one side of her, which makes the whole thing sag like a hammock. Freeman practically falls into the crack between two seat-cushions and ends up slumped against Lanie.

Don't touch me, she says, and scooches over to the opposite end of the couch.

Freeman picks himself up out of the crack and says, Did you say the whole subway was down?

Lanie turns her head slightly to pierce him with an ice-cold stare.

They had shuttle buses running between stations, she says. Do you have any idea how many people you inconvenienced?

I don't know. Depends how long the power was out.

How long? says Lanie. She grabs the armrest and spins round to face him. Her eyes are no longer glacial, but wet and fiery.

Freeman knows where she's going, and his stomach tight-ens. It's like watching an oncoming train wreck and being powerless to stop it.

Come on, Lanes, he says. Don't cry. Nothing bad happened.

Nothing bad? Lanie glares at him, but her puffed eyelids make her look like she's squinting.

Freeman focuses on an invisible point in mid-air, zoning out the restless images on the TV screen along with the news-caster's nasal whining. It's easier than asking Lanie to turn down the volume, or pass him the remote. After seventeen years, Freeman has learned there are non-negotiables, and this is one of them. Another being the fact that when Lanie decides to have one of her meltdowns, there's nothing he can do except what he's always done.

He takes a deep breath, and another swig of Coors.

Seventeen years ago, Lanie was doing her Certificate in Project Management at George Brown, and Freeman was newly arrived in Toronto. He'd taken the Greyhound from Winnipeg for a construction job that never materialized. By then, he'd already rented a closet in a ramshackle rooming house above a junk store on Bathurst Street, and couldn't afford a return ticket. A few days later, Lanie landed in the room beside his, after evacuating her ex-boyfriend's apartment.

After one sleepless week of listening to Lanie crying and ranting all night on the phone about some douchebag called Jay, Freeman knocked on the cardboard-thin wall between them and asked if she wanted to step outside and smoke a joint with him.

When Lanie moved out of the rooming house to live with some friends, Freeman thought that would be the end of their liaison. But she told him he was the best listener she'd ever met. Then she graduated, got her first job and her own apartment, and Freeman moved in with her.

Sometimes, Freeman wonders if life without Lanie might be, well, calmer. But what would he do with no one to soothe and talk down from whatever histrionic peak she's worked herself up to? Like the time she got fired from a job she'd been complaining about from the day she signed on. Instead of celebrating, she freaked out because now who was going to pay the rent? Freeman didn't have an answer for that, but he managed to convince her that things would work out. They'd get through this together. Everything was going to be fine.

It was true enough: Lanie stopped crying eventually and found herself a new job. Meanwhile, Freeman continued to eke out his contribution from odd jobs picked up around the neighbourhood, through a handwritten poster taped to trees and telephone poles with his phone number at the bottom on tear-off tabs.

PAINTING, YARDWORK & REPAIRS

GOT A PROBLEM?

LET FREEMAN FIX IT!

(NO JOB TOO SMALL)

Lanie thinks he should work on his marketing, maybe get one of those free websites. But then he'd have to charge more and he'd lose some of his regulars. And he wouldn't want to get too busy. Lanie's living proof of the price of success, and managing her stress is a full-time job—one he actually finds rewarding, though he'd never say it out loud.

The worse Lanie gets, the better he feels.

So when life crushes Freeman under its dirt-encrusted boot and grinds him into the ground like a half-burnt doobie, he asks himself what he'd do if the same thing were happening to Lanie. He tries to imagine himself safely outside his own life, dispensing advice. But his mind refuses to fall for that trick—Lanie wouldn't last a day in his shoes.

She'd never stand for penny-pinching homeowners who expect him to risk life and limb cleaning their eavestroughs, up on a ladder with no one to stand guard because they won't hire an extra pair of hands. In the case of the client whose dog peed all over the red cedar fence Freeman had just installed, before he had a chance to stain it, Lanie would never have spent an afternoon scrubbing out the stench with vinegar—and the owner had the nerve to complain he couldn't smell the cedar. As for the family who denied that their "mouse problem" was actually a raccoon infestation, she'd have refused the job outright on the grounds of animal cruelty. In the end, Freeman managed to trap one of the babies in the recycling bin and presented it to the Wildlife people. He has no idea what they did with the critter, and he'd rather not picture it.

Where is that smarter, wiser Freeman when he needs him? How come his shining alter ego only comes charging to the rescue for Lanie's battles? Why, when anxiety courses through him like a flooding sump pump, can't he locate the water main?

The worst part is having to hide it. If Freeman so much as hints that he's having a rough day, Lanie pounces on him, claws out. He's clearly depressed; he should see a shrink; he's radiating negativity like a cellphone tower and it's freaking her out. Lanie herself isn't depressed, of course. She's just a highly sensitive person with standards, which means she can't help noticing what others gladly ignore. People will take advantage of that.

So Freeman keeps his mouth shut and his problems inside. And whatever was bothering him cools and diffuses. His stomach settles. The lake of roiling lava recedes over time, leaving a small black stone lodged somewhere beyond repair.

The first time this image arose in Freeman's mind, he wondered if it was a premonition—his grandmother used to have those. What if the vision meant he had kidney stones, a hernia, or even cancer?

Freeman's loathing for the medical profession is comprehensive. He's not about to set foot in some pretentious, overpaid doctor's office to talk about an imaginary illness. If he drops dead one of these days, at least he won't see it coming.

As for his grandmother, she was always a bit "out there." She ended up in a home, too arthritic to shuffle her tarot cards, surrounded by residents whose deafness immunized them from her apocalyptic predictions.

An hour later, Freeman's tried every trick up his sleeve and Lanie's still mad. He's apologized, promised to buy dinner at Famoso's, tried tickling her. Finally he gets up, stands behind her, and tries to administer a neck massage. She shoves him away.

Freeman shakes his fist at Lanie's unyielding shoulders and says, Can't you just be happy for me?

Lanie snorts derisively. Happy for what?

I could have got hit by a train and ended up in hospital without a health card.

You would have deserved it.

What?

You put your life at risk of your own free will—you deserved to die.

Freeman can't believe what he just heard.

Jeez, Lanes, he says mildly, you're worse than the cops.

Transit security had detained him for over an hour in a windowless office. When the two police officers finally arrived, Freeman had joked that they must have been held up by a subway delay. He'd got a wry grin out of the younger one, at least. The officers were thorough and patient in their questioning, and listened intently while Freeman described his escapade in detail. He felt a rush of pride as he explained how he'd vaulted the safety fence while holding on to the handrail with one hand, then landed lightly on both feet. He recalled the care with which he'd picked his way through the dark, using the flashlight on his phone.

The police had written it all up in a report, pausing to add footnotes when Freeman recalled some minor detail. Then they'd let him go with a four-hundred-dollar fine, which they told him he could appeal in small claims court.

It felt anticlimactic.

Freeman's never been to small claims court. He wonders if it's a real trial, like when his buddy got busted for driving with an expired license. A group of them had rented an SUV and headed to Montreal for a guys' weekend, taking turns to drive. They got pulled over on the way back, near Oshawa, while Shaun was in the driver's seat. The interior stank of booze, sweat, and pot, and Freeman half-expected the cops to arrest all four of them. Months later, when word got out that he'd forgotten his license at the Airbnb, his buddy tried to guilt him into splitting the paralegal fees. Even though the ticket had been dismissed by then. Freeman suspected that Shaun's wife was behind this. And the reason why he'd stopped coming out to Friday nights at Paupers.

Maybe this is karma, catching up with Freeman. If he'd chipped in to help his buddy, maybe none of this would be happening. He can't afford to hire a paralegal, but that's all right—he's not afraid to defend himself. When it's his turn to speak, he'll tell the jury just what he, Emanuel Freeman, thinks of the city. They make you pay for buses that never show up. Then half an hour later, they send three buses at once. They cancel trains for no reason other than that the driver got stuck in traffic, driving his Lexus to work. The transit system represents everything that's wrong with the world—the reason why honest workers like Freeman get lost in the cracks, stuck in a thankless cycle with no end in sight.

But even if he tells that story, nothing will change.

All that matters now is that Lanie's okay, because if she isn't, there's no hope in hell for Freeman.

Why, Manny, why? Lanie says softly, between strangled sobs. What's that?

For the second time tonight, Freeman can't quite believe what he's hearing.

Why did you do that selfish and stupid thing? she says, turning her tear-streaked face to his. She doesn't even sound mad. Did you do it on purpose?

Why? echoes Freeman. He thinks: because I got sick of waiting. Because I needed to change trains at St. George, and walking along the tracks to Spadina was the most direct route. Because there weren't that many people around and no one was watching. Because I saw it in a movie once. Because I was running late, and wouldn't have made it in time to get my health card anyway.

Now that he thinks about his reasons, they don't add up. Every point he might make seems mind-numbingly trivial. Not worth the argument. Certainly not worth dying for.

It was stupid, Freeman admits.

Are you sure you weren't trying to kill yourself? Lanie is insistent. Did you want to die?

A vision of death appears in Freeman's mind: a deep, velvet emptiness in which there appears, in the infinite distance, one flickering star. The darkness is reassuringly absolute, restful even. Yet somehow he finds himself drawn like a moth toward the light—just like he's heard it described. Why is that? What is it that makes us willing to risk being burned, to die trying rather than meekly close our eyes?

Of course I didn't want to die, says Freeman. I'd never see you again, and what would you do without me?

He goes to sit back down beside Lanie and the gelatinous seat-cushion rolls him halfway into her lap, but she doesn't push him off.

What reason did you give the police? Lanie asks. Did you tell them you were running late?

Of course not! He places a hesitant arm around her shoulders, and she lets him.

What I told them, Freeman says with pride, is that I saw a lost dog, but when I got down there I realized it was probably a rat—or a terrorist.

You're terrible, says Lanie. But through her tears and mussed-up hair, Freeman sees the beginnings of a smile.

Relief courses through him. He tries to hold back. He's got to stay strong for Lanie.

It's all right my love, says Lanie.

Somehow, she's got her arms around him. Somehow, she's the one holding him tight while his eyes brim over, his face contorts and his shoulders shake. What's wrong with him? Is this some kind of fever? From somewhere close by, he hears an ugly, persistent noise. A cross between a stalled engine throttle and a cat in heat.

You gave me such a scare, Lanie says. I was so scared you'd leave me, I was so scared. But you're safe home now.

Freeman's breaths return to him in irregular, heaving gulps. He manages to sit up and look at Lanie, her red-rimmed eyes bright with care and concern. But when he tries to speak, that choked, grating sound begins again.

Shh, says Lanie, shush now, everything's going to be all right.

She pulls him to lie down with his head on her lap, and Freeman lets her. He curls up on one side, his face to her belly, and lets all tension ebb away. When the seasick feeling subsides, he turns his head and looks up. Lanie has dozed off, her neck bent forward, chin to chest. Her brow is smooth and untroubled. Her face is so close he could reach up and kiss her.

Better turn the TV off so it won't wake her.

He tries to get up but Lanie's cradling him with both hands, and her fingers refuse to be prised off. So he lies there and stares at the ceiling fan, which he realizes has been on this whole time, quietly doing its job. He's never realized how fast that thing spins, or how potentially lethal it is—like the wheel Sleeping Beauty must have killed herself on. Or was it the spindle ... It was one of those fairy tales his grandmother used to tell him, with the details altered to suit her own views. The person who gives Sleeping Beauty the spinning wheel usually gets blamed for her death. But it was her own darn fault for not reading the manual first. And like most princesses, she probably had long, flaxen hair, which she didn't bother tying up. Anyone could see what was coming.

He reaches an arm up toward the fan, but he's too far below it to feel its breeze.

The tunnel was kind of cool though, he says quietly. Do you know what it reminded me of?

Lanie's still asleep.

Freeman continues: It's like those people who say they've died and come back to life. They say they saw a light at the end of the tunnel, and that light was heaven. But what I want to know is, if that's true, then how come they're not dead? Unless there's a light at both ends of the tunnel, and they had to pick one. That must be it. We choose to come back to earth because the light of living is brighter.

Parlour

For three years, Tulene has had the bathroom to himself. Still, he keeps a milk crate stocked with the essentials just inside the door to his room, for easy access. If Old Chow were to find Tulene's toothpaste beside the bathroom sink, or his towel hung on the bent nail poking from the back of the door, he might demand more rent.

Old Chow is the probable author of the handwritten sign: *This Is A Unisex Washroom. Keep Clean!* On Tulene's own door there's a tarnished brass number *1*. At the opposite end of the corridor is a third door—unnumbered, bolted, padlocked, the mail slot nailed shut. Behind that door, Granny Chow passed away a few weeks after Tulene took up residence above this Chinatown junk shop. Tulene used to detect the odours of stale bread and sour milk wafting down the corridor, or when he approached the toilet, its seat left lowered, the lid up. He would hold his breath and wrench open the tiny window beside the shower stall, and the smell of sewage and rotting vegetables would float up from the alley below. He never met the old lady.

Last Friday, Tulene came out of his room as usual, locked it carefully behind him, and nudged open the bathroom door. The air was damp as a dew-drenched morning, except it was four o'clock in the afternoon. Droplets glistened everywhere.

Tulene pulled aside the shower curtain, printed with a pattern of mallards—some flying, others short-necked, chests puffed, stiffly planted on their sheer, slightly undulating ground of waterproof plastic—and there, coiled around the drain, was a long black strand of someone else's hair. Tulene picked up the hair with two fingers and dropped it in the bucket beside the shower stall.

Back in his room, he realized he'd forgotten to brush his teeth but he couldn't turn back now. He was already late for work.

Early on Sunday morning, Tulene returns from his Saturday night shift at the parking garage. He pauses at the bottom of the stairs and hears the click of a lock or latch—or perhaps it is just the creaking of beams and joists. He goes upstairs, looks up and down the corridor, and sniffs the musty air. Without turning on the light, he can see that the bathroom window has been left open. Grey dawn has begun to trickle in, along with the aroma of overflowing garbage bins two floors below.

It can't be Old Chow's doing—it's the middle of the month. He's barely set foot in the place since the old lady passed, perhaps for fear of an indignant ghost. Tulene pulls the window shut and tiptoes away from the bathroom, down the unlit corridor. He gets within a few feet of the unnumbered door and stands still, waiting for his eyes to adjust. Out of the darkness, images appear: reddish paint peeling in fine, curled flakes; a padlocked bolt. Except instead of a wooden board nailed roughly to the centre of the door, the mail slot is now clearly visible—a prim, pursed mouth.

Tulene crouches down and places his ear against the metal lip. At first there is only silence; then he hears a faint rustling, a whisper so slight it barely displaces the dead air. Tulene listens until the blood throbbing in his ears becomes a roar.

He hurries away for fear that someone should discover him like this, deaf to every sound but his own heart.

Mondays through Thursdays, Tulene is free—that's the best part of the job. Cooped up in the collector's booth counting change for twelve hours, being served dirty looks by drivers who think the downtown parking fees just add salt to wounds bled dry by a night on the town. No one else wants the weekend shift. The second-best part of the job is between ten and two, after the last of the overdressed big-timers and their underdressed dates have strutted off toward the BOA Lounge or Empire Cabaret, and before they stumble back for their Volvos and BMWs. That's four hours' paid study time, so long as Tulene can stay awake.

On Monday morning, Tulene gingerly eases open the bathroom door and notices that someone has left a whole roll of toilet paper in the toilet paper holder. Each quilted sheet is decorated with a delicate floral print. He takes a corner between finger and thumb, and it's almost as thick and soft as the fleece scarf he lost last week.

He's still thinking about the toilet paper when he trails downstairs after breakfast, pulling at his freshly washed beard; there's barely enough to wind around his fingers. It hasn't been trimmed since his birthday and the tufts sprouting from his cheeks and jaws are as mangy as the dealer's dog.

On the front doorstep, Tulene scans sleepy Chinatown streets, thinks about lighting up. Quitting smoking is harder than growing this beard.

"What's shaking?" says Duchamp from the doorway of his shop.

He holds a mug of coffee in one hand and scratches his belly through a threadbare tank top. A forest of curly hairs pokes out above the neckline.

"Not much," says Tulene.

"Watcha got there, man?" Duchamp looks him over lazily, like a well-fed wildcat.

"I got nothing." Tulene holds out empty palms. His backpack stays snug against his shoulder blades.

"Me neither." Duchamp laughs, gargles coffee. "I got nothing. I'm nothing. I'm useless." He kicks at an armless doll that has rolled off a mound of junk and is lying across the threshold.

By day, Duchamp's place is junkyard heaven. Nights, he pulls the batik-print curtains across the storefront window and thudding bass shakes the block right up to where Tulene sits at his kitchen table, head bowed over a doorstop-worthy tome entitled *Advanced Calculus*. Tulene hopes the insistent beat will hammer the formulae into his head—formulae that make little sense today but might one day bridge the way to a job at a big corporation, or teaching grade school.

"Hey," says Tulene. "Did someone move into Grandma Chow's old flat?"

"Did Old Chow scrub the cat-piss from the floorboards, or give that dump a good airing after they found her body, five days rotten?" Duchamp snorts. "Man, that dive is a case for Public Health."

Tulene remembers the smell, like sewers and the back of the butcher's shop mixed together. After paramedics broke down the door and manoeuvred the body downstairs on a stretcher, the smell penetrated every corner of the building and lingered for a week. Tulene rolled up his bath towel and wedged it under his door. He held his breath each time he bolted across the corridor to the bathroom. He flung open the tiny window above the toilet, and the smell of the garbage below seemed almost sweet.

"Guess you're right," Tulene shrugs. "Well, I gotta go."

"Hot date?" Duchamp slugs back his coffee, drags a hand across foam-flecked lips.

"No." Tulene looks down at the wave-like patterns of salt stains on his battered work boots, and the frayed shoelace that has already come undone. "Just meeting a friend. For study."

At twenty-two, Tulene is the oldest student in the GED class. For this reason, he doesn't mind being teased about the scarcity of his beard. At least it erases three to five years off his face.

Every Monday afternoon, Tulene shoves his notes, unfinished homework assignments and *Advanced Calculus* into his backpack, and goes to meet Junjun. Junjun is taking his GED because his Chinese high-school grades can't be translated into Canadian. Tulene hopes that at least he is glad for a chance to practise his English.

In Junjun's small, quick hands, the calculus problems dissolve like snowflakes falling on the Red River, months before it freezes over. Fingers dance across calculator keys; pen-tip glides dragonfly-quick across paper. Tulene can barely restrain himself from applauding each time Junjun completes a particularly tortuous problem, writing the solution triumphantly on the answer sheet, spearing the page with a final decimal point and throwing down his pen.

"$x(t)=c_1+c_2t+c_3et+Atet+B\cos t+C\sin t$. Easy."

"$B\cos t+C\sin t$," repeats Tulene, enchanted.

"In China, this is for babies—we already do in Grade Eight."

Then painstakingly, in broken English, Junjun guides Tulene through each knot he has just unravelled, stopping often to ask, "Do you understand?"

"Yes," says Tulene. "You're so good at calculus. You'll get a really good job one day."

Back in October, Tulene was sitting alone in the cafeteria of the Adult Learning Centre, slumped before an empty paper plate, a crushed can, and eleven open packets of Hellmann's Real Mayonnaise.

"Excuse me. The coffee here—is good?" Junjun had said, in Mandarin.

Tulene looked up uncertainly.

"Sorry, so sorry," said Junjun, in English.

Tulene's mouth was full of day-old bagel, or he would have said it was okay. Most people thought he was Chinese—if not wholly, then in general. He was in fact part Chinese, an indeterminate percentage, on his mother's side. That part was mixed with some Métis, also indeterminate. Someone had told him that Indigenous people might have come from Mongolia; they'd walked to this continent across the Bering Strait. Did that mean the Métis were partly, almost Chinese? Tulene wishes he'd figured this out before his mother died. They'd lived together above the noodle house where she washed dishes for seventeen years. At the time, it didn't seem to matter where they might have come from. After the funeral, he dropped out of school for the last time and moved a block away, to the room above Duchamp's.

"My name is Junjun," said Junjun, and held out his hand, even though Tulene's fingers were clearly daubed with mayonnaise, which he hurriedly rubbed onto his jeans.

"Tulene," Tulene mumbled, wishing he had not drained his Pepsi so fast. He was having trouble swallowing the last bites of half-chewed dough.

Junjun looked at Tulene with an expression of delighted surprise. Tulene would soon learn that this meant Junjun had not understood.

"My name is Junjun," Junjun said again, phrasing it this time to sound like a question.

"Tulene," Tulene repeated, almost choking in his efforts. "My name is Tulene."

"Too-lean," said Junjun gravely and inscribed it in meticulous black ink in his leather-bound notebook.

Junjun is on a mission to find the best coffee in Canada. Tulene has never liked the taste of coffee. It's disappointingly bitter, unlike its enticing aroma. Each Monday, Junjun arranges to meet Tulene at yet another deli, greasy spoon, or espresso bar. He photographs his order and posts it on his blog entitled: *Winnipeg's Best Western Coffee*. He labels the pictures with date, time, star rating out of five, and the name of the roast: Three Sisters, Kicking Mule, Blonde Costa Rican.

At first, Tulene was baffled by Junjun's fastidiousness. "They're just names," he objected, "They don't mean anything."

Junjun kept writing but his eyebrows rose in question, and Tulene hurried to repeat himself.

"They—are—just—names," Tulene said, stopping between each word so that they no longer ran together, merging into an indistinct whole.

"Every name has meaning," Junjun replied, now animated with real surprise. "Your name very unusual, must have special meaning, no?"

Tulene started to disagree, then stopped.

"Tulene" was simply his mother's misspelling of a place-name; really two places mixed up in her mind that she had once heard on a radio programme about the Canadian North. Villages so isolated that sometimes in winter, mail and groceries could not be flown in for weeks. Villages as magical as the ones in Tulene's picture books, filled with heroic princes and beautiful princesses. "Tulene far, far away," she told him. "Always cold, always snow." He spent years perusing their outdated and dog-eared *Maps of Canada* until he finally discovered, tucked away in the Northwest Territories, the hamlets of Tulita and Deline. He ran down to the kitchen, thrust the map in front of his mother and pointed, "Look, Ma!" His mother glanced down, frowned, and returned to peeling the veins from a plate of snow peas. "Maybe," she said. "Maybe. Too long ago now."

Since Parlour Coffee opened on Main Street last year, Tulene has often walked past on his way to class. Outside the tall windows, customers in black suits and sunglasses soak up the sun on storefront benches. They sip at takeout cups and cigarettes and ignore the proximity of the Woodbine Hotel.

Junjun says Parlour reminds him of Vienna, which he visited with his parents on a tour-bus vacation. He told Tulene about a city where the buildings were as ornate as the cupcake confections at Lilac Bakery. Painted brick, marble columns, three opera houses to choose from. After the performance, the applause lasted for fifteen minutes. The rafters rained roses on the Italian prima donna. Junjun hadn't understood a word.

There is no such thing as pop, or juice—or coffee, for that matter—on the gilt-framed chalkboard behind the marble counter. Tulene scans the list of unintelligible names and settles on an espresso, which at least sounds like an English word. The clerk rings up his order: an espresso at Parlour costs three times the price of a regular cup of joe. Tulene has never paid much attention to price lists; has in fact avoided looking too closely because Junjun always offers, even clamours, to buy. He should have waited outside on one of those uncomfortable-looking benches made from upturned wooden crates, sanded and varnished. But what if they'd mistaken him for a homeless guy from the Mission up the road, and chased him off?

Tulene starts to count out the change in his pocket. He pats down his jeans again, hoping to hear the clink of coins he might have missed, his palms growing moist, just as Junjun arrives.

"Café au lait," says Junjun to the clerk and places his hand over Tulene's hot, shaking one. "Let me pay, please."

Junjun thinks nothing of slapping his textbooks down on the countertop beside the window and slipping onto a leather-covered barstool, beside patrons toying with smartphones and retouching makeup with mirror compacts, while they trawl the street for eye candy or a reciprocal appraisal. Tulene squeezes into the free spot next to Junjun but can't help elbowing his neighbour, who doesn't flinch, but fixes Tulene with a gaze so steely it pierces the fake leather of his favourite jacket—a motocross style popular the year he left school.

Espresso sloshes from cup to saucer. Tulene feels the blood flooding his cheeks and vows never to come back to Parlour. What's wrong with meeting at the cafeteria?

"Best coffee in Canada," Junjun smiles, and raises his glass.

Tulene's espresso is bitter, unfamiliar. He tries to savour it, allow the burning brew to linger in his mouth, educate his taste buds in European sophistication.

These days, Tulene's tutor, who scowled and shook his head at him last year, now smiles even when Tulene slinks into class late, eyes downcast, and heads for the back row. But what Tulene is grateful for, more than good marks and free coffee, is that Junjun has never once made a disparaging remark about Tulene's mutt heritage, let alone his complete ignorance of any one of the seven or so dialects of the Chinese language. "Good," Junjun had said. "I only want to speak Canadian English from now on." *Now we are both foreigners*, Tulene had thought. But that was absurd, in a country pieced together from the leftovers of displaced cultures.

What a nonsensical language English can be. Take a word like *unisex*, implying a creature neither man nor woman, but one sex. Yet it is not the same as *hermaphrodite*—a word Tulene remembers from a fifth-grade biology class where earthworms in Plexiglas containers writhed over and under each other in a tangled knot. Tulene could not tell their heads from their tails, let alone whether they might be male or female. To his relief, it transpired that they were both.

At least no distinction is made between masculine and feminine words. Tulene hadn't thought about this until Junjun asked, "So is coffee a girl or a boy?"

"What?"

"In Chinese, some words have the symbol for a girl, or a boy."

Tulene remembered French classes, the baffling illogic of *un* and *une*, *le* and *la*.

"It's neither," said Tulene. "In English, coffee is just a thing. Only humans and animals are male or female."

"What about plants?" said Junjun. "Plants are living too. And coffee is made from beans."

This made Tulene's head spin. "No," he said, finally. "Coffee is just a thing. It does not have feelings."

Today, Junjun rushes through the steps and Tulene struggles to keep up. He completes three quarters of the assignment, then says, "You understand?"

"I think so."

"You finish by yourself," says Junjun. "The rest is easy."

Tulene's eyes widen but Junjun is already on his feet, shrugging his hooded Roots jacket back onto his shoulders.

"You didn't finish your coffee," says Tulene. The café au lait is cooling in its glass, a film of milk-grease congealing on top.

"It wasn't that great," says Junjun.

"I thought you said … " begins Tulene, but Junjun is already backing away, eyes downcast, as if scanning the floor for something slipped out of his pocket—loose change, or a phone number scribbled on a napkin.

At the same time, Junjun's neighbour lays down her mirror compact and turns her attention to her hair, held up in a high, blonde chignon from which wisps have begun to escape. As she pulls pins from her head, the tendrils loosen and multiply into a thick, shimmering cascade. Junjun swerves, too late, as pale gold strands linger on his shoulder and graze his cheek.

"What about English conversation?" Tulene has to raise his voice to reach Junjun, thrown off course by the sudden intimacy.

"No time," calls Junjun. "Not today." He ducks as the blonde gives her head a final toss, unleashing a brittle, powdery perfume.

It must be her hairspray, but it's not a scent Tulene can place. He recalls the old bathroom cabinet, the cracked mirror on the sliding door behind which his mother stored a few simple items: toothpaste, deodorant, extra bars of Irish Spring.

"Okay." Tulene coughs. "See you next Monday."

Junjun looks confused for a moment, as if they have not been meeting every Monday since October.

"Parlour?" adds Tulene, helpfully.

Junjun is still shuffling backwards toward the exit. "No, not Monday. I have a dinner."

"Dinner?"

Junjun hesitates. He returns, places a hand on Tulene's arm.

"She is a really nice girl," Junjun says quietly. "Emma. From our class. You know her?"

"Emma," says Tulene. The hairspray is making his eyes water. "That's a nice name."

"See you later," says Junjun and walks out of the big glass doors, down Main Street, where the cars are honking and crawling, packed together two by two.

Tulene stares at Junjun's half-empty glass for a long time. It looks like a cross between a beer stein and a champagne flute. Then he pulls it discreetly toward him. He raises the glass and sniffs at the floating milk skin.

The taste is not half as bitter as the espresso. *Milk and sugar*, Tulene decides. That's the trick, the way to make this foreign coffee more palatable.

For a while after his mother's death Tulene had considered heading north, packing a sleeping bag and hitchhiking as far as there were still roads. He knew that the places he was looking for were only reachable by plane. He would have to start off by finding work, with cargo perhaps, helping out on the runways. The plan took on the significance of a pilgrimage. Then his grief subsided. Now the desire to travel at all was something buried that only stirred infrequently, like a hibernating creature.

When Tulene gets back, Duchamp is still sitting on the stoop, scratching his belly, cigarette dangling from his lips, ash dropping. Instead of a chipped mug, there is now a bottle of Budweiser by his feet.

"You're back early."

"Yes," Tulene mumbles. "I need to study."

"Don't work too hard," says Duchamp. "Want a beer?"

"No, thanks." Tulene can feel himself begin to redden as if the beer were already in his belly, firing up his insides.

Duchamp has the bottle to his lips when he lowers it abruptly and calls, "Party at my place tonight. You should drop by. Never know who you might meet."

He winks, and Tulene turns away to hide burning cheeks. All that caffeine is making his heart pump twice as fast.

"Maybe later."

"Take it easy, man," says Duchamp as Tulene starts up the stairs.

On the landing, Tulene pauses. The bathroom door is closed, but that's to be expected. He's even heard it slam shut while he was sitting at his kitchen table. That's the problem with old buildings—the draft always finds a way in.

Tulene approaches and studies the handwritten sign. Below the words *This Is A Unisex Washroom*, penned in thick black marker, are Chinese symbols in blue ink. He has always assumed that those complex characters are a direct translation. For the first time he realizes he has no way of knowing for sure. He listens at the bathroom door for a minute, then two, then three, and hears nothing. Through the crack beneath

the ill-fitting door, and under his own door, too, seeps a
weak late-afternoon light. Only one doorway remains dark.
As he pads down the corridor, his footsteps accompany the
beating of his heart.

Standing before the dead woman's door, Tulene raises his
fist and strikes. He stands and waits. When his legs tire, he
leans cautiously against the door. When it does not budge,
he sets his shoulder against it. He struggles silently till he
remembers the mail slot. With hesitant fingers, Tulene traces
the edges of the metal flap, daring himself to lift it by just
a crack. He takes hold of one corner and raises it. A slip of
paper slides out and flutters to the floor.

Tulene leaps backward, letting go of the flap, which clangs
shut. Surely the keeper of the mail slot is about to wrench
open the door and come roaring out! He holds his breath
and shuts his eyes hard; he no longer believes this will make
him invisible, but the habit still offers comfort. When he
finally dares look, there is only the familiar darkness. He
crouches down and rakes the dusty floorboards until his
fingers close upon a folded slip of paper, thin enough to fold
twice more and hide inside his fist.

Passing the bathroom door again, Tulene sees that it was
not closed after all; it is open by a hair. He extends a tenta-
tive finger and the door swings open before he can touch it.

The air inside is as fresh as a spring day after the rain.
Tulene smells flowers but cannot name them. Jasmine?
Camellia? There was a row of glass-stoppered vials on his
mother's dresser, labelled with these names. As she sickened,
Tulene shook their contents onto cotton balls and dabbed
them on her shrivelled throat from where the coughing came.
No matter what he did, the room's smell of vomit and bleach
was stronger.

Are flowers male or female? They are neither, or both—they have pistils and stamens.

The draft comes from a door beside the shower, a door that Tulene is almost certain has always been locked before, half-covered by the plastic curtain. Now it is wide open. Tulene had assumed it hid a broom closet or electrical panel. He now wonders if this door once opened onto a balcony or a fire escape torn down years ago, for there is no ledge beyond, just a sheer drop.

Tulene looks down at his clenched fist, the knuckles so white that it seems the colour of his bones is showing through his skin. As he watches, his fingers uncurl and the slip of paper opens its folds, perched in his palm like an origami bird. Sunlight pierces it and reveals a whole line of writing in reverse on the other side—blue ink, on paper lightly wrinkled by the sweat of his skin.

Slowly, as if looking in a mirror, Tulene struggles to decipher the message. What at first appear as random shapes and swirls gradually become letters, then the beginnings of words, but still Tulene cannot make sense of them. They are like fragments from a story lost to childhood, one that his mother might have read to him, whose meaning is now closed.

The shower curtain floats fitfully in the breeze, flapping against the empty stall. Tulene stares at the printed ducks—the blithe, airborne ones and the staunch, standing ones, determined to stay rooted even though the ground beneath them is slipping out from under their feet, has already slipped, and is fluttering toward the open door. He holds out his hand.

The breeze seizes the corners of the folded slip and whirls it outside, above the alley. Just before it flits out of sight, Tulene clearly glimpses blue letters ablaze, suspended in mid-flight:

When I hold you, I hold everything that is—
Tulene reads swiftly, without effort. He can almost be sure he's read them correctly, the afterimage of those words still hanging before him in the empty air.

The Stain

INT. THE STARLET'S BEDROOM, BEVERLY HILLS—DAY

Is the stain in the centre of the rug?
 Is the rug in the centre of the room?
 Both are technically possible. And technically impossible
to verify without being there.

INT. THE STARLET'S BEDROOM, PASADENA—DAY

I am not there, at The Starlet's Mansion. I'm at home—my
real home—watching this week's episode of *Whatever
Happened to Kim Cattrall?* I am not Kim Cattrall, but
like her, I am Canadian. Originally from Vancouver, now
living in Pasadena. This show is not about Kim but about
a twentieth-century starlet with similar hair and physiog-
nomy making her twenty-first century comeback on reality
TV. Before The Starlet, my best-known role was that of a
French supply teacher in *Degrassi Junior High*. I managed
a convincing accent but I am not bilingual. Contrary to
popular belief, not all Canadians speak French.

Today is my birthday—on screen and in life. I asked to take
a "personal day" as soon as I heard they were planning a
special edition in honour of my fiftieth (not my real age). It
will be my stand-in's most high-profile episode yet—she'll
be competing for screen time with The Starlet's celebrity

guests. Last month, in episode six, "Not the Wedding Planner,"
I personally arranged for the rental of a two-hundred capacity,
luxury white marquee with both air conditioning and a
furnace (in Hollywood, the weather's as fickle as the fame).
Catering by Daniel Bouloud. No gifts, please. My birthday
is an occasion to give back to all those who've created The
Starlet with her four-decades-long-and-counting career (three
decades, officially).

The first person I put on the guest list was my accountant.
Where would I be without him? He of the classic fit Dockers
khakis. I didn't expect him to show, so imagine my surprise
when he walked into the banquet hall just now and sat down
next to Jon Bon Jovi.

But I am getting ahead of myself. Everything moves so
fast in television. Especially in The Starlet's world, where
events occur in real time without pause. Feel breathless yet?
Unlike our competitors' offerings, each episode of *Whatever
Happened to Kim Cattrall?* is live-streamed. We are the real
deal.

INT. THE STARLET'S BEDROOM, BEVERLY HILLS—DAY

Today's episode began when The Starlet woke from her afternoon siesta. I do love a siesta, but I have never managed to fall
asleep at The Mansion. Not even when the cameraman hides
behind the curtains, his equipment-laden contours draped
in floor-length, Delft-blue damask. The rug in The Starlet's
bedroom is salmon pink, with an ornamental rose border,
because that's what the producers thought The Starlet would
order on The Shopping Channel.

INT. THE STARLET'S BEDROOM, PASADENA – CONTINUOUS

At home—my real-life, mid-century ranch in Pasadena—my bedroom is decorated in shades of grey. I like to say *Fifty Shades*, to make the boys blush. As if anything shocks the young these days. The truth is, I gave my feng shui consultant strict orders that the only thing this bedroom was expected to deliver was a good night's sleep. TV life is exhausting. There's always a party at The Starlet's Mansion, which might explain the stain, except the party hasn't started yet.

INT. THE STARLET'S BEDROOM, BEVERLY HILLS – DAY

The Starlet climbed out of her American Empire mahogany four-poster, a vision of pink silk and platinum curls. That's all you need to sell this adult fairytale. A glimpse of semi-sheer, nipple-grazing kimono; an artfully teased, bespoke hairpiece (filched from my personal wardrobe); a passable imitation of my signature hip-wiggle as my stand-in sashays over to the French windows. Cue a shot of her silhouette against the Santa Monica Mountains. No closeup today, because makeup and prosthetics can only do so much to suspend disbelief. Everyone knows: The Starlet is me.

The camera panned over the still-sleeping form of The Starlet's latest conquest. A tangled mop of surfer waves. Tanned posterior contoured in rippling shadows. Dimples of Venus tapering toward gluteal dunes. Bedsheets draped like a Michelangelo nude, cascading to the floor. And then the rug in all its glory, filling the screen like a rising flush.

That's when I saw it: a peach-hued blemish, about the size of a pitcher's mound relative to the size of the rug. Right by the West Elm sofa.

INT. THE STARLET'S BEDROOM, PASADENA—DAY

Everything looks bigger on TV. What you see on your screen
is a distortion of reality, caused by an accident of lighting
and viewpoint. The same theory could apply to the stain
itself. Perhaps it's not a stain, but a back-brushed patch of
high-pile carpet. Come to think of it, the area did appear
slightly raised. Which is what made me think of a pitcher's
mound in the first place (the bedroom being comparable to
a baseball diamond). In television, perspective is everything.

By my calculations, the stain is right in the centre of the
rug. Unless they moved the sofa. Or they could have moved
the rug off-centre. But why would they? A rug that size isn't
an accessory. It's in every shot, setting the tone. The eye-wa-
tering flamboyance that, in the first series, had me looking
down each time I walked into that room, no matter how dis-
tractingly handsome my partner *du jour*. The director didn't
mind. He said that this small, involuntary gesture—a tic,
almost—was quite sweet. It showed equal parts detachment
and vulnerability. It made The Starlet more relatable.

You wouldn't think you could get used to a rug like that.
But it faded into the background, along with my nerves. In
a series as authentic as ours, it makes sense for the lead to
evolve.

I should be glad of a reason to replace this gaudy and dated
design feature, but that's not my job. The rug has become
part of the package: pink, plush, and eager to please. It's
suggestive of all the things that can, do, and must happen in
The Starlet's bedroom. It's what viewers want. Why fix a tried
and tested formula? It may be stained, but it's not broken.

The director is legally obligated to inform me about the posi-
tion of the hidden cameras. But it's impossible to remember

every obscure location, especially after a few drinks. Did I mention that every day is a party at The Starlet's Mansion? As a result, the director is the only one who knows where the cameras are hidden, and which one gets the best footage.

Of what? you may ask.

To which I say: Have you been living under a rock with no cable? Do the ratings a favour, and tune in while you can.

Anyone who's had as many lovers as The Starlet could write a book. I still pinch myself when I remember that her suitors audition for the privilege of airtime with me. The Starlet is officially bisexual. The casting director is a gay man. Compared to the brawny young studs he routinely corrals from back alleys and drinking dens, my female lovers have, so far, been a disappointment. Call me old-fashioned, but I can't abide piercings and tattoos on a woman.

Still need a teaser? It's safe to assume that most of the action centres on the bedroom. Did you catch what I just said? Centres. Here I am in front of the TV in my cashmere sweats, with a bottle of Veuve and the best West Coast weed south of Portland, and I'm worrying over a damn stain.

That's what's centred in my bedroom right now. And I'm not there.

INT. THE MARQUEE—DAY

A note on the soundtrack for this edition. Jon Bon Jovi's people said he would only attend off-duty and incognito— for a fee. This despite the royalties he receives each time "You Give Love a Bad Name" gets airplay during a romantic encounter at The Mansion. My PA honed her bargaining chops in Hong Kong street markets but failed to out-haggle Itzhak Perlman, even after I sent a personal note explaining that, when the melatonin and valerian root don't work, I

cue up the soundtrack to *Schindler's List*, and his haunting
violin lulls me to sleep. Which is why the musical act for
tonight was not my choice: an androgynous, part emo, part
goth singer-songwriter in black leather moto pants and a
T-shirt that reads Love Won't Save You. I must admit that
the casting director's appreciation of the male form is more
inclusive than I thought.

The entertainment has a seat at the table with the other
guests, but is expected to perform between courses. For
all his attitude and eyeliner, he's really just hired help. He
approaches the mic grudgingly each time, convinced that no
one at this party will have heard his self-titled EP, let alone
understand the subtle, introspective lyrics; their obscure ref-
erences to the Ramones and Jane Birkin. His name escapes
me, but I did look him up on Wikipedia, in case I am ever
asked to recount the events of my fiftieth birthday party.

The same reason I am watching this charade at all.

Who am I kidding? The tabloids claim I'm inches away
from being replaced, in future episodes, by a body double.
Apparently, I need to drop pounds or drop out of the prime-
time race.

I'm sure the producers are behind this—a bunch of pil-
low-paunched misogynists secretly threatened by the idea
of a woman their age being sexually liberated. What they
don't know: the only way I can reach orgasm is on camera.
Everything else is acting.

We're at half-time and the action still hasn't left the marquee.
Isn't it time we got back to the bedroom? What will my
viewers think?

But wait—here's our sullen, pale-faced warbler scraping
back his chair and heading for the exit (not before casting

a mournful, craft-beer-worthy glance back at his half-full bottle of Corona Extra). There's The Starlet—all black shades, platinum tresses, and pink couture—whispering in my PA's ear before slipping out through the clear, plastic door panels, ahead of her troubadour.

The move seems surprisingly spontaneous. He's hardly lover boy material, more like an understudy for Edward Scissorhands. The off-script effect is heightened by the crew's delayed reaction. By the time the cameraman makes it to the edge of the marquee, his targets have already circumvented the swimming pool and are crossing the patio.

INT. THE MANSION—CONTINUOUS

We catch up with the lovebirds as they stumble back indoors, across the deserted atrium. It's the perfect sequence for a spot of shaky cam, which also captures the toe-curling awkwardness of this mismatched couple. I'll admit that our recent nomination for Outstanding Technical Direction seems to prove the Emmys aren't rigged in *all* categories.

Up the marble staircase (no time to linger on the gleaming map of forked and twisting paths), to the mezzanine lined with closed doors.

Where do they think they're going? The canopy bed in the guest room isn't set up for aerial filming. Where's the director when you need him? Probably on top of one of those perpetually miscast, nose-ringed nymphets.

I'm wondering how the crew will improvise their way through the ensuing build-up to climax, when the door slams shut behind the happy couple.

INT. THE MARQUEE—CONTINUOUS

My accountant waves a cigar in one hand and a spoonful of brandied peach parfait in the other.

INT. THE STARLET'S BEDROOM, PASADENA—CONTINUOUS

What kind of show do they think this is? I would never close the door on a camera! Not even in the bathroom. That's why they have those trite disclaimers: *Viewer discretion is advised.* It's not my place to be discreet—that's called *editing.* Being The Starlet is a full-time job! To be there, on screen, willing or not, is what it takes. No matter what they say behind my back, in boardroom meetings, on their petty and pernicious Twitter feeds, when The Starlet is in the room, so are the cameras. What the camera sees is all there is.

And now I am gripped by an unsettling apprehension that by being absent from this star-studded happening, I have made a terrible mistake. Because of me, this episode will not peak. The Starlet's whole raison d'être has been pulled out from under her. In its place is white noise, a roar of jumbled whispers: *over the hill, out of touch, a travesty.*

I have become invisible.

It's all I can do to stop myself from grabbing my Ray-Bans, jumping in the Lexus, and driving straight to The Mansion, over the speed limit and under the influence. But that would be madness. The Starlet never travels without her chauffeur, and right now he's at the marquee, on his fifth Gatorita of the night. I made sure that my hard-working staff got VIP passes.

Why am I still watching? Truth be told, I can't find the remote. Is this, too, what my viewers are thinking?

INT. THE MARQUEE—NIGHT

The cameras have settled like flies around the table where my accountant is holding court. I can see the pained smiles of his captive audience, to whom he is expounding his grand theory of microeconomics. They are nodding their heads in apparent agreement while secretly thinking, Who invited this goof? I find myself silently willing him to climb up on the table and break into a soft-shoe shuffle. But the camera zooms in for a candid interview. You can practically count the veins in his nose.

"Before tonight," my accountant says, "all I knew of The Starlet's legendary parties were the photos in *People* and *Hello!* When I received the invitation from her PA, I thought it was a practical joke. Tonight, my life has changed."

His words bring tears to my eyes. I no longer regret inviting him. The thought actually crosses my mind: I can die happy now. On reality TV, that is.

INT. WHOLE FOODS MARKET—DAY

One of the things I appreciate about living in Pasadena is that no one knows me here. After a lifetime of celebrity, being photographed makeup-free on my Starbucks run is the least of my worries (being chased by paparazzi is so early-2000s). Back then, they gave you a role, and when the cameras stopped rolling, you stepped out of that bodysuit and went home. These days, I can stand in line for my organic aloe and wheatgrass smoothie, dressed in head-to-toe Gucci, and no one asks what I'm doing "in character," just me and my iPhone, no camera operator in sight. They're too busy pretending not to ogle Kourtney Kardashian—not a local!—second aisle to my right, through that forest of selfie sticks. When the show first started,

I used to go as myself, on my days off. But it left viewers confused. I could see it reflected in their fingerprinted Ray-Bans: Who came first—The Starlet, or the idea of The Starlet?

EXT. THE MANSION—NIGHT

The birthday party is winding down, and the driveway is lined with limos. The Starlet is still in the guest room. It's embarrassing, really. After this episode, people will think that a) I am the kind of person who leaves her own party to have private intercourse with a complete stranger, and b) I have terrible taste in music. As for The Starlet's taste in home decor, there's still time to change that.

INT. THE STARLET'S BEDROOM, PASADENA—NIGHT

It has been almost an hour since I spotted that stain on the bedroom rug, and I am starting to think it was always there. Which begs the question: Why didn't I notice it before? I am a fastidious person. Even if most of the time I spend in that room, I am looking at the ceiling.

Most probably, this stain is the type that's barely noticeable in real life. It just doesn't translate well to screen. The fact that it's one shade lighter than the carpet itself makes me think it's the result of over-zealous cleaning. The actual cause could have been anything. Coffee. Wine. Personal lubricant (the silicone-based, long-lasting kind).

Murder. That'll boost ratings. The shape of the stain is nothing like a human body, but who actually believes what they see on TV?

FADE TO BLACK.

Nights in Arcadia

It's not because he looks like Benicio del Toro, or acts like he thinks he does. She just can't resist grown-out mullets, excess under-eye baggage, and rare sightings of full-fleshed lips through weeks-old facial shrubbery.

"I'd like to paint you," he announces, seconds after mispronouncing her name and reaching across the bar for a handshake like crumpled vellum.

"In the nude," she adds, beating him to it, or so she hopes.

He laughs shyly, twirls his soul patch between paint-stained fingers. "Well, sure, if that's what you're into."

Typical artist, already absolving himself of responsibility. If only he'd absolve her too. There's no shortage of benches in the park round the corner, even after midnight when the drunks drift in to roost. But she wouldn't turn down a nice soft bed with an extra body to keep it warm. Even better if it comes with a set of lips like del Toro's.

"Just kidding," she backtracks. "We can keep things PG-13."

He doesn't look as disappointed as she'd hoped.

Lighten up, loosen up, let it go. That's what they all said. Her mom. Her drama teacher. The neighbour's goose-eyed daughter. Adolescence was the one subject she couldn't master. Critical thought was the enemy. Who knew that learning the body could feel so counterintuitive? After a decade of rooting out and exterminating every last instinct for shame and inhibition, she feels like a wing nut hanging on to its bolt by one groove. Maybe half a groove.

"So, Kyoto, what do you make of the music?"

"It's Coyote." Does she (still) look Japanese? Has he seen through the green eyes and sun-streaked hair to commonplace self-disgust, all dressed up as something less embarrassing, pitiful or pathetic, if not quite sexy? Most men don't have an eye for coloured contacts and seamless extensions, balayage highlights that cost her monthly food allowance (thank God for dumpster diving). But most men aren't artists, not in her circles at least.

Being a muse might appeal if the pay's any good.

"Ky-o-tee," she enunciates at read-my-lips half speed, then braces for routine interrogation. How did she get her name? She must have made it up, because what parent would give their kid a name like that? *None of your business, asshole!*

This time he hears her, above the thrash and grind of some unbilled indie rock trio headbanging away on the distant stage. One hour before closing, the dance floor's littered with broken glass and straggling solos.

So maybe the Asian stereotyping was an honest mistake. He gets extra points for not saying it's a beautiful name. She'd like to think she's a hard-nosed realist. It takes nerve to do what she does. Live light, keep moving, holding her small losses close to her heart like a pack of well-worn baseball cards—the player, the poet, the jock. *Collect them all!* Their worth fluctuates depending on the time of day, or month, and her degree of drunkenness. The idea was to trade up, or sideways at least, but it seems she's on a losing streak.

"That's a name I haven't come across before."

She says, "I can't stand it."

"What?" He brushes curtain bangs out of his eyes, tucks them behind his right ear. Long-lobed, with thick-rimmed pinna curling inward, toward the mysterious canal that leads to the inner ear. No apparent hirsute obstruction, but the lighting's on his side.

"You asked if I like the music."

It takes him at least five seconds to muster a belly laugh. Abrupt and a little grating. Maybe she was wrong about the ear canal. Either that or it's the mark of a real *artiste*—especially at the wunderkind level, they're more or less dysfunctional.

"And here I was thinking your boyfriend might be in the band."

"Why? Is yours?"

Another guffaw. "I don't mind it," he says. "They sound like they know what they're doing. They sound pretty good to me."

And if a thing is good, does it mean you have to like it? If it's good for you, will it also be good to you? She hasn't gone looking for "good" in a long time—it gets in the way of runaway sunset horizons.

It was meant to be a weekend getaway, not the Great Escape. Early August, island living at the boyfriend's parents' cottage, just like a Chatelaine spread. Moonlit skinny-dipping and beer breakfasts. A coming-of-age road trip—for the boyfriend, that is. Coyote had been on the road, slumming it in backwater Ontario small towns, ever since dropping out of Grade Twelve right before exams. She was planning on getting her course credits after she went home.

They had a falling out on the drive back to the burbs, over whose turn it was to buy cigarettes. Ended up hitchhiking to Napanee and spending the night undetected in a church basement—her first. Too spooked to sleep, she stayed up copying the gothic designs off stained glass windows on the insides of deconstructed donation envelopes. Doodled a python wrapped round a crucifix, painted it the next day in dollar-store acrylics on a Salvation Army T-shirt.

Later that summer, a girl at a Montreal drum circle bought the python shirt off her back. It was the fastest five bucks she'd ever earned, not counting back-of-the-bike-shed blow jobs.

"Cool T-shirt, by the way." He says that while looking straight into her eyes, even though the design in question is located significantly lower. Match point del Toro.

She raises her glass to hide her smile and drown the hopeful butterflies. Let him be the talent around here, let him try to figure her out. His guess is as good as hers.

Celebrity holds (almost) no magic for her. She's watched exactly none of BdT's movies. But now that she's sitting next to the man himself—he hasn't told her his real name, and she's not going to ask—she feels like she's back in her teenage, suburban bedroom, surfing Hollywood insider blogs, filling blank journal pages with the screenplay of her future life.

It's just another phase, this utter boredom with guys her age. Nothing to do with her parents. The words "father figure" make her toes curl, and not in a good way. She's not looking for a sugar daddy either, doesn't have the nose for it. They're an acquired taste and she's never had a whiff of Dom Pérignon.

He's leaning—swaying?—toward her, elbow patches mopping the beer-soaked bar. There's a chip in the frame of his eighties YSL glasses. Could he be the genuine, vintage article? A bearded, retrofitted hipster with baby-soft hands, probably incapable of changing the washer on a bathroom faucet—not an issue when the closest you ever got to having your own was a porta-potty beside a construction trailer; exactly what you'd expect from shacking up with a summer fling past his expiry date.

This guy might just be too drunk to tell her leg from a bar stool's, considering how many times her knee has nudged his. But just as she's given up, legs crossed primly under the bar, his hand finds its way to her thigh, slides toward a tactical rip in her Free People jeans. Skin on skin, thermal shock—he pulls back, breaks contact. She didn't think she was *that* electric.

He pulls a vibrating phone out of his back pocket and squints over his glasses at the caller ID. *Adorable!*

"Do you mind if I take this?"

Sweet of him to make her feel like she matters. Two can play that game.

"Who is it?" His wife? His lover? A teenage daughter asking to borrow the car?

"My broker. Wants to meet up for a nightcap."

Novel proposition: an artist with money. Must be an amateur or a genius. Sip at the beer you hope he's going to pay for, sit pretty, stay hopeful.

If all else fails, she's only blocks away from her friend's warehouse loft and the couch where she left her backpack—*go ahead, look through my dirty underwear, nothing worth stealing.* By the time she walks back, barefoot, wedge heels swinging from one hand, maybe the party will have died down. It's the annual pre-Halloween costume-a-thon, hosted by Drew of the freakishly successful line of monogrammed man purses, and this year's theme is White Trash. Coyote opted out on the grounds that almost everything she owns is black. Just back in town after a two-year hiatus, her capacity for irony's not what it was. Besides, a crowd's a safe place only when you're anonymous.

Sam spent their weekend in paradise consumed by the develop-
ment of his burgeoning pectorals. Bench-pressing a homemade
barbell cobbled together from his dad's old golf cart tires, while
reclining in a deck chair on the overgrown lawn. He lay there, up
to his elbows in dandelions, refusing to lift a finger in the direction
of the lawnmower. She envied that trick he had—that all boys
have—of opting out of humanity at will. Of making the rest
of civilization recede into utter irrelevance, tuning out entirely
until Coyote herself disappeared. When he held her in his arms,
which were criss-crossed with thick, pulsing veins, she imagined
a gradual electrocution. Her brief life's experiences slowly erased.
What would it feel like if the tables were turned—to hold this
amount of power over a person? She's tried doing it to herself but
you can't will yourself into oblivion, you need someone else to
help you forget. To override your reality with theirs by the sheer
force of boy–girl attraction.

Del Toro drains his glass, lowers it, sets it down on the slick
bar top. *Was that a white glove or a gauntlet?* He clears his
throat, fiddles with his wayward forelock.
    "Uhh, got any cigarettes on you?"
    "What kind of cigarette?"
    "Any kind you're offering."
    "Now you're talking."
    The following events occur in quick succession like unre-
lated newsflashes. The empty glass taxis along the bar rail
and is stopped by a soggy coaster. The artist's hand bypasses
her knee, closes around her unfinished drink, and ever so
slightly displaces it. And when he lurches to his feet, she sees
he's left something pinned under her glass: a slip of green
plastic paper, one corner fluttering in some unfelt breeze
like a baby flipper waving SOS.

"Settle up for me? I'm going to visit the little boys' room."

The little boys' room. Would those words in any other place or time have set off the radar that warns you're speeding toward a fork in the road: fight or flight?

She's got most emergencies covered by the contents of her jet-bead-and-tassel-trimmed purse. Tools of the trade, and not just rubbers: pepper spray, a pocket knife, a ring of lost keys to doors she'll never open. On starless nights she clutches the keyring so ridged shafts poke out like bared teeth between her knuckles.

The little boys' room. Who says that anymore? In this paranoid age of too much information and massive assumptions. How could anyone be this tone-deaf?

She can't watch the news because she can't unsee those faces: the missing girls and invisible women. She could be one of them. Maybe she is already. Who will find her, if she can't recognize herself?

What's she doing here in Arcadia?—a wannabe speakeasy, no-cover dive where cover bands go to die. Is this the afterlife? The girl she used to be wouldn't have been caught dead in a place like this, rehearsing lukewarm small talk with a stranger whose street smarts are so outdated, he's entrusted his tab to her. She could signal the bartender like a dutiful girlfriend, hope there'll be another surprise plot twist before evening's end. But there's still a third of a pint left in her glass and she'd better not chug it back in a hurry—not on an empty stomach. So what else is she going to do with her hands? What else could she do at the sight of that bank bill, green and crisp, like a bite out of Eve's apple?

It's not a stop-light-red fifty. The fact that it's only twenty is practically a sign. Feed it to your hungry purse, slide off the barstool, try not to trip on your way out the door. What's another grain of sand in your shoe for each free mile? No time to stop and ask if it's worth the blisters. Isn't that how pearls are made? Smile, you're back on the road, where you belong. Any moment now.

Now when she thinks of Sam, she sees his eyes in the rear-view mirror of his dad's old three-door Jetta. Squinting at something on the road ahead, brow set in a James Dean scowl. Meanwhile Coyote's channelling Marilyn in a strapless white number, with scuffed black combat boots and Lolita's sunglasses. Back then, every day was a movie shoot for a black-and-white classic-meets-retro-kitsch mash-up.

"Got any smokes?" Sam never talked much but when he did it was a mumbled growl. Puberty hit late, not that he'd admit it.

Coyote, from the passenger side, did a little shake-and-shimmy. She couldn't see herself in his mirror but she had an inkling he could. Something about the whiteness of his knuckles, both hands steering. Sunlight bouncing off her glitter-dusted shoulders.

Sam kept scowling. Who knows what he was thinking? Maybe nothing at all. Not words, that's for sure. Just guttural animal sounds.

She reached two fingers into her underwired cleavage and fished out a crumpled white paper tube. In the mirror, Sam's eyes did a blink and a sideways jig.

"Only if you buy me a new pack when we stop for gas."

The eyes narrowed but didn't flicker.

"You've got to be kidding."

Coyote pouted. "But it's my last Lucky Strike."

"Didn't hear you complain about the case of Labatt's you put away last night."

This from the boy who said he couldn't have just one beer or he'd get a headache. He'd cheered her on, ripping the ring pulls off

*her empties and tossing them into the fire pit, slapping his knee
each time she hiccupped: "My girl belches like a cross-country
trucker!" How could he take down the thing that made you proud,
revoke the prize, and shame you?*

"You said to help myself."

"Sure I did. Maybe I should take my own advice."

He reached over, plucked the cigarette from her fingers.

Her skin burned, as if he'd ripped off a layer.

He was rummaging in the console. "Got a light?"

*It was all she could do to stop herself from ramming her knuckles
into the mirror—not that it would have worked anyway, knowing
her luck. The thing would probably swivel on its black plastic arm
and evade her, just like every other target of her emotion.*

*"Stop the car," hissed Coyote. She had a handful of white seer-
sucker balled up inside one sweaty fist, ready to shred (what was
one less ruffle on a dress with more tiers than the prom queen
she'd never be?). Her other hand was already on the door handle.
"Stop or I'll jump."*

"Close the door."

*He wasn't even looking at her. One summer of love and he
thought he'd seen it all. What would make him look again?—the
way he used to, in the early days, when they were both younger
and less savvy by three whole months, and possibly a little less
stoned.*

*"Calm down," said Sam, her first real lover, her only friend. "It's
just a goddamn cigarette."*

Even at that age, she knew a killer closing line when she heard it.

Once outside, though, her legs won't work. They bear her
a couple of blocks east, then collapse in an unlit storefront.
Far enough to throw a guy off her trail. Not too late to turn
back. *It's only a twenty.* She must be losing her edge.

Whatever happened to those Robin Hood days, when stealing meant more than survival? A badge of honour, brigands' blood firing her veins. This was in her tomboy phase, before the age of rejection. Her initiation: a packet of gum drops filched from the tuck shop—some boys in Grade Five put her up to it. A false promise, the first. A losing game. Maid Marian was just as much a crack shot as her merry counterparts, and they still passed her around. Time for some karmic redistribution. The tide of fortune practically owes her a turn.

Starting with the backlog of unfilled orders in her Etsy shop. Tiny Dancer Designs: upcycled clothing, one-of-a-kind creations. Please note, your order may take up to six weeks' processing time (especially when she's between couches). Her design of the month (last month by now): two mermaids sixty-nining in a tai chi symbol. Maybe she should offer a refund on (delayed) shipping costs before her store gets roasted by bad reviews. Panhandling pays better. It slows her down, this desire to leave a mark, even on something as trivial as a printed crop top. Evidence of her fleeting passage through this world of dreams and shadows. You can't escape capitalism when almost everything that's free is illegal. At least she can't be accused of selling out.

Relax, lighten up, light another cigarette. No point planning further than your next pack of smokes. Be here now: Queen Street West on a Wednesday night, Pearl Jam rip-offs ringing in her ears. Slumped in the shelter of a piss-stained doorway, legs folded under, knees going numb, while dead leaves and litter chase each other in a cheesy ice-dance number under the streetlamp spotlight.

Coyote's fumbling through lint-lined leather pockets for a lighter when a flame appears out of the darkness with a hand attached to it. *Benicio?* He's mostly backlit, a figure in a snow globe filled with yellow leaves. The past will always catch up with you, but it's usually not *that* fast.

"Cheers." The hand hovers inches from her face. "Just what I needed."

The flame goes out. It's just her and a potential rapist on a deserted street.

"You know you shouldn't smoke." A country ballad voice— whisky and rye.

"Why not? We're all going to die." She dislikes country music as a general rule.

"Sure. But first, it's going to get a lot worse."

"Go ahead, surprise me." She yawns. Smoke in his face. Dragon's breath.

He backs up, steps right under the lamplight. Wire-rimmed glasses. A salt-and-pepper crew cut. Shapeless black parka. Maybe it's ironic. Maybe he just doesn't care.

"Trust me," he says, "I'm the patron saint of smokers."

You know you've hit rock bottom when you catch yourself believing in redemption.

"Is that why you carry a lighter?"

She's sorry the next instant, watching his smile shrivel like a salted slug.

"Wait, don't go. I know who you are. You're a warrior of light. You've earned your angel wings through denial and self-sacrifice. You've battled the demons of addiction and now you've come to save me. But I'm not ready. I'm not even drunk. See, I can stand up. Come help me get up."

She casts grandiose circles in his direction with her burning cigarette. The lit tip releases a powdered flurry.

He doesn't move. He's probably trying to decide: *Is she worth the effort?*

"Come help me. Please help."

A crumb of ash lands in her eye and now she's tearing up.
The wall behind her feels like ice through the leather. She
should have finished her pint. But what she really needs is
something stronger.

Where's the patron saint of vodka?

Funny how the closer he gets, the less she can see of his
features. He crouches down beside her, and his face is all
shadow.

Doesn't matter. She knows who he's not.

*Aerodynamics were against her. Wind pushed back against the
Jetta's door, narrowing that glimpsed sliver of endless blacktop. So
she climbed out the window. Ripple Sole Docs all over his prized
fake leather interior. That ridiculous dress billowing up over her
head. Sitting on the ledge, the rolled down top edge of side glass
carving a groove in the backs of her thighs, she pounded her fists on
the sun-baked roof and cursed Sam with every name in the book.*

*She wasn't expecting him to stop. Not really. Hadn't he prom-
ised to take her street racing? Speeding together at the brink of the
possible, toward the promise of the invisible. Wasn't that what
the future was supposed to be?*

*Passing drivers honked and hollered, "Get off the road!" She
waved back and gave them the finger.*

*The highway flashed by in blurred white and yellow stripes.
The smell of melting tar and burnt rubber. If she leaned back
just so, face to the sky, would the wind catch her and keep her
from falling?*

"What the fuck are you doing?"

*A hand grabbed her ankle and pulled. She lashed out with her
other leg. The Jetta swerved. Her ankle was free again.*

"Get down, bitch! Do you want to die?"

Coyote raised both hands in the air and howled like full moon night in Lake Country.

"Easy there, you all right?" The patron saint of smokers leaps forward to catch her falling cigarette at the exact moment that Coyote's eyes snap open and one leg kicks out. One moulded plastic wedge heel strikes brittle tibia bone, inches below the knee, missing its target.

Caught off guard, the victim yelps and drops the cigarette. It fizzles on the ground like a lit stick of dynamite.

"Sorry," Coyote gasps between gales of wild laughter. "I'm out of practice." A side kick from the ground is hard enough to pull off even when you're not wasted.

He's a safe distance away now. A black and white portrait by streetlight: the cracks in his carapace where shadows pool, the white bristles in his day-old beard, the roughened mole nestled on his chin.

"Are you all right?"

What's he talking about? Isn't he the casualty around here?

"Do you need help getting home?"

His persistence might be charming if he didn't seem so desperate.

"Here, take your cigarette."

The giggles are ebbing, but her shoulders keep shaking like stunted wings.

"You can't stay here all night."

"You got a better idea?"

"Come on. You need to get up."

She's trying to get it together. Can't he see that she's trying so hard she might actually take off, if she wasn't so afraid of heights? It's been a long time since she last dreamed of flying.

The lamplight's a distant glow, the night doesn't seem so cold anymore. She'd close her eyes and drift away if it wasn't for this weight on her shoulder, pinning her down.

"Don't touch me!" Coyote writhes free and springs to her feet, fully awake now.

This time, he doesn't retreat. "Hey, calm down. I won't hurt you." There's a flatness to his voice that tells her he's been here before.

"What are you," she snarls, "an undercover cop?"

In another place and time she might have said those words in a different tone, like an open invitation.

"Listen," he sighs. "It's not worth it. I was angry with my ex-wife for seventeen years."

He's the perfect age, of course. Can she, would she, stomach the bedside manner?

"And then what happened? You discovered yoga? Crack cocaine?" She likes playing dress-up as much as the next person. Handcuffs and stethoscopes, yes please. But a Good Samaritan…?

"You can't go through life laying blame for all your past regrets."

So much earnestness, she has to look away. When in doubt, have another smoke. She opens her purse and takes out her cigarette case. A flash of engraved silver, mother-of-pearl inlay, and velveteen interior.

"I used to have one of those," says the patron saint of smokers, wistfully.

"Maybe it was this one."

"I sold mine."

"I stole mine. He was asleep. I wanted something to remember him by." She pulls out a fresh cigarette, puts it to her lips. *"Je ne regrette rien."*

"We've all done things we're not proud of."

He holds out his lighter before she can ask, cups the flame with his free hand. His eyes are obscured by fingerprints and reflected light. She wants to tear those dirty glasses off his face and stomp on them, grind them to dust along with all his good intentions. How dare he think he knows what she needs as well as what she wants.

Coyote leans forward, fumbles for the zipper on his waterproof shell. He flinches but doesn't stop her. His breaths are harsh and jagged. Fried onions, black coffee, sour milk. The zipper seems to be missing its tab.

"What are you doing?" His voice is thick with hope, or smoker's phlegm—but he doesn't smoke.

She gives up on the zipper and pulls his jacket open with both hands, slips the cigarette case in his inner breast pocket, then closes him up again.

"You're right," she says. "I really should quit."

Now run. Take to the streets before he can stop her. Wings on her ribbon-wrapped ankles. She is Aeon Flux in civilian disguise, sprinting to the end of the block then cutting through a side street, turning down back alleys at random to evade capture. The smudged stamp on the back of her hand is a fading passport. There's still time to make it back to Arcadia.

In the end, Sam pulled over onto the verge, crossing three lanes of highway traffic like a getaway driver in a Hollywood heist. He'd barely braked before Coyote jumped out, skidding on gravel, slamming the door so hard it might have been the force of her fury that sent the Jetta tearing off again, wheels spitting grit in her eye.

"Good riddance, asshole!" Her Marilyn dress a torn white flag, already sorry, begging to be rescued.

Sure enough, the Jetta hadn't crossed the horizon before she'd flagged down a Jeep driven by a couple of local boys on their way to a shift at the ONroute Wendy's.

She never looked back. Hitchhiked west till she was as far from home as she could get without crossing an ocean. On the Pacific coast, revolving seasons blurred into each other. No past, no future. Saltwater, superior weed, and oxygen-rich altitudes could make a girl forget the one-eyed bird woman, or the man with his IV drip bag taped to his bike helmet, at the mobile soup kitchen on Seymour Street. She would outrun aging. Hopping barefoot down rainy Robson Street to save her Converse sneakers, setting up camp outside The Bay, hungry but hopeful, not minding the omnipresent odour of wet dogs and damp sleeping bags, and the Siberian-husky-and-golden-retriever-mix fur that clung to everything.

That was the phase when the only item of clothing she owned that wasn't black was her pink lace-up corset. That was the phase when she thought that's what an artist should look like. She knew it was over the day she woke up wondering: what goth in their right mind would adopt not one but two rescue dogs—one three-legged, the other with arthritic hips—both long-haired and snow-white?

This time, she bought a Greyhound ticket. Spent three days curled in a window seat with a coverless copy of The Beautiful and Damned. She, who never used to need recovery time.

The dogs stayed behind with the bass guitarist of a death metal band from South Surrey—they're probably deaf by now.

She hears the music before she reaches the fogged-up door. The sound of Arcadia. Alice Cooper fading into the Red Hot Chili Peppers. The bouncer lets her in with a curt nod. No questions. Anyone who hangs around bars and nightclubs after hours gets used to seeing ghosts.

Moving shapes emerge from the shadows as her eyes adjust to the dark. The band's packing up, dragging equipment across the stage, and shouting to each other as if they're underwater. The bartender's collecting empties. She's probably missed last call but that's okay, this'll only take a minute.

There's a forlorn, half-empty pint sitting at one end of the bar. She hopes that it's hers. How long was she gone? Her swollen fingers sift through her purse and locate the twenty, smooth to the touch. She pulls it out and puts it back where it belongs, face up, glossy and green as a royal frog.

A figure appears at her side, pulls up a barstool, and waits to see if she'll stay. She doesn't turn her head. She plays a guessing game. Is it a) the artist, b) the psychiatrist, or c) none of the above? She listens for a voice she might recognize.

The boys from the band traipse by, arms laden with gear. Green, red, and blue lights paint their faces pale and unlined. The lie of agelessness: a trick of bad lighting, questionable booze, and classic rock. Tunes that sound familiar even if you've never heard them before—it's the analog synths. These kinds of songs were written way back in the last century, before Coyote was born. Like the one that just kicked in. A drum-kit backtrack, steady and sober, aloof as a lone wolf on patrol. A cool, baritone croon like a whisper in your ear. The voice of someone who knows you.

And in that moment when her guard is down, the man beside her catches the flicker of interest in her eyes and takes it as a sign. He holds out his hand and says, "Hi, I'm Sam."

A wash of slithering snare and shimmering hi-hat diffuses the doubt in her.

"Nice to meet you, Sam."

The taste of his name in her mouth is instantly unsexy. It's not his fault. Lumberjack shirt, belted jeans, thick fingers around a pint glass. Don't look back. Focus on the music, which after all is the loudest thing in the room. That hypnotic voice, slightly mocking. Sweet interrogation with a London lilt. A voice that could pull you under and make you stay. The singer's asking her if she can hear him. To give him a nod if she can.

Sam must have thought she was nodding at him, because he raises his glass and says, "Your turn."

She has no idea what he means. But that's okay. The voice is telling her it knows how she feels. It says she's about to feel better. She hopes so, because the look of guileless expectation on Sam's face is starting to unsettle her.

He smiles again, as if to reassure her that whatever his intentions, they're fully appropriate to the present situation. "Aren't you going to tell me your name?"

She sighs with relief—a familiar script. "Coyote."

"Sorry?"

"I know what you're thinking. You think I don't look like I'd have a Japanese name." She doesn't know why she said that. She's too tired for this game.

"No, no," says Sam. "I wasn't thinking that. I mean you look—" His pale eyebrows knit. He pushes his drink aside as if it's responsible for his confusion. Beer sloshes to the rim but miraculously doesn't spill.

The music fills the room and softens every sharp corner. It draws you in, promising protection. It seeps inside and finds the places that hurt. It coaxes confessions—but who to tell?

She gives him a small, close-lipped smile. It's all the encouragement he needs.

"My ex-wife was Japanese, actually, believe it or not."

He must be older than he looks.

Coyote sits up, blinks her eyes awake, tucks a flyaway strand behind one ear and says, "Tell me more."

Sam's words come slowly at first, between sips. As the glass empties, his words quicken. "I suppose I've always been drawn to outsiders, that I'll admit. People out of their element. Homeless in a way, I suppose."

Is it the music, or something he said? Somehow, the way she feels is exactly what the lyrics describe. Like sleepwalking in someone else's body—numbed out, far out. The calm, slow thrust of each inevitable beat. All her past lives converging to this moment, distilled to a tireless pulse. Relax. In the future, there'll be time enough to say: "That first night we met, I wouldn't have pegged you for a romantic." Maybe she'll even tell him about Sam the First and they'll have a good laugh. If they ever get there.

"She said she never wanted children. Turns out she just didn't want them with me."

"Maybe," says Coyote. "Maybe she changed her mind."

She's not taking sides. She's just keeping her options open. Will he understand? And if he does, will it be because he's clever or kind?

"What about you? Any kids in your future?"

A perfectly reasonable question, given the way the night's playing out. She'd tell him if she knew. It'll be years before her biological clock takes over, or so she's heard.

"Sorry, didn't mean to pry."

He looks away quickly and reaches for his near-empty glass. Puts it back down, wipes his hand on his jeans, and runs red-knuckled fingers through baby-chick hair. His hair is so fair it's white where the light shines through. She wants to reach out and touch it too, while he's not looking. He doesn't remind her of anyone, yet everything about him—his barrel chest, the hint of a paunch above the waistband, the way the tops of his ears taper back against his head like a puppy's, signalling fear or submission—is already familiar. If she sits still and waits, maybe he'll get used to her.

He lifts his head and darts her a hummingbird glance, eyebrows raised. The years multiply across his forehead. He looks down again and the years are erased.

Maybe he changed his mind.

But that look. Still a surprise, no matter how many times she's seen it before. A prom date mumbling into his non-alcoholic beer:

"You want to get out of here?"

"Sure. Your place or…?"

The drummer shambles past with his drums stacked in his arms like a wedding cake. "Hey man," he says, "Give us a hand with that door, would you?"

Sam leaps to his feet and bounds ahead so that by the time the guy gets to the door, it's wide open and Sam's waving him through like a smiling doorman. The cake teeters, navigating the doorway, then pauses. Sam bows his head, listening—she didn't realize he was so tall.

The next track's all lonesome guitar, twelve-string chords shaking the empty club. The same voice, now urgent and raw. And suddenly she realizes, of course she knows this song, and the one that was playing before. The bartender must be streaming the entire *Greatest Hits.* It's one of those bands so famous, you only learn their name years later, after a lifetime of recognizing fragments wherever you go—from the radio of a passing car, the closing credits of a TV show, or an elevator you rode for a floor or more before you noticed it was going in the wrong direction. Wherever you are, the music follows. And when you finally notice the song that is playing, you realize that what you thought was the first time is only the latest in a finite number of last times. You realize you are not immortal.

Sam, alone in the doorway now, turns back to call something out to Coyote. His lips form the syllables, but she can't hear a word.

"What?" she mouths back.

She hopes he said "I'll be back," or "Wait for me," perhaps. But really, it could be any combination of three syllables—she thinks it was three—and now he's turning away, ducking through the open door. She feels the draft from off the street. She wants to call him back before he's out of sight, to make him turn once more, just to know she can. But when she tries to summon his name, her throat constricts. Her animal body balks because it knows that word belongs to the past.

The other day she pulled on the same sweater she wears every day and found a strand of white hair, two inches long. *Was it dog or human?*

She knows how this song will end: with a sound like wind tearing the eardrums, as if the band recorded it on a spaceship hurtling away from earth, into outer space. On the original album, this track transitions smoothly into the next so you can't tell them apart. But on the *Greatest Hits*, it cuts off abruptly as if the spaceship's trajectory was suddenly diverted by alien forces.

If he doesn't come back soon, will she still know him?

Sam's name escapes her now. It slips off her tongue and under her breath, down the empty bar, a note without a song. In its wake is the blue flame of his gaze, clear as that vision said to appear before death: your own life speeding toward you, for the first and last time. She'll hold on for as long as she can.

Breathe Now

1.

So many zippers, so little change. Wolfgang scrounges for loonies among the lint and crumpled rolling papers, tracking a hopeful jingle. But it's only his keys turning up in a forgotten pocket of his black parachute pants, the ones so voluminous they could host their own rave.

Going home is never easy. Clambering up and down snow-choked stairwells, rapping numb-knuckled on a series of seemingly identical front doors. Only the numbers keep changing.

The irregular alarm of a barking dog. A muffled curse from far away, inside.

The keys blink coyly from his ungloved palm, as if daring him to figure out what to do with them. Might as well pick up some smokes at the all-night depanneur.

Blue streetlight—the only colour in a black-and-white world. Wolfgang squints skyward, half expecting to glimpse frozen stars. White on white. Where are his sunglasses when he needs them? Ground to glitter-dust on the dance floor.

Into his open hand, snowflakes fall like quarters and dimes.

2.

The locations of the parties keep changing, which is under-standable, though for all Wolfgang cares it might as well be the same derelict warehouse transplanted wholesale to yet another unclaimed corner of the washed-out city.

The same nonsensical password.

The entrance through a broken window.

The concrete floors riddled with rubble and puddles of strange liquid.

The dull groove of dark music.

It can't last. Only a matter of time before the cops move in like fungi spreading on the rotten tree trunk beside the railway tracks in the scrap-metal sculpture park.

The city starts shrinking the moment he stumbles out onto unfamiliar streets, wandering until daybreak hits like a subcutaneous injection. Sooner or later, he'll run out of detours. Eventually, one of his keys fits one of those doors, or maybe someone forgot to lock it. He's back inside the rooming house. That second-floor corridor lit by a trickle of greenish light from a single, fly-encrusted wall sconce. No choice but to flounder toward the octagonal vanity mirror glinting above the farthermost door, a false beacon daring him to cross the threshold.

If only there was no afterlife.

3.

Wolfgang manages to get the door open without looking inside (these days, there's no telling what he'll find). He sticks his hand in first, gropes around for the light switch, flicks it on, and opens his eyes: nothing. He flips it the other way and his pupils recoil; his arm flies up to block the vision.

There's a woman sitting at his kitchen table, drinking out of his favourite bowl—the one with Winnie-the-Pooh on a background of cracked blue.

"What are you *doing* in here?" Wolfgang takes a step back and the peeling outsole of one soaked sneaker snags on the toggle end of a bungee-cord hem. He stumbles backwards into the corridor, arms out. The door slams shut.

Next time he'll keep his eyes open. If this is a dream, there's no point trying to sleep.

"I knew you'd be back." The woman at the table sets down the bowl and smiles. Her front teeth are grey and gapped. Something limp and yellow dangles from the gap.

"How did you get in?" He takes one step into the room, keeping the door open with his other foot.

The woman looks down at the bottom of her bowl. As if there are tea leaves down there. As if she could read them.

Already his eyes are closing, losing focus. Wolfgang gropes for the worn top rail of one of those old classroom chairs and drags it toward him before he collapses.

Across the table, a grey and yellow blur: wrinkled chicken skin.

"Aren't you happy to see me?"

He doesn't answer. He has the feeling she's about to tell him something he already knows.

4.

The girls at school don't interest him. For one thing, they're French. Wolfgang didn't start going to École Saint-Esprit until Grade Three. No matter how hard he scrubs at his Anglophone accent, they keep reminding him that he'll never be a real Montrealer. "Where's your *maman*, Wolfie?" they chant. "Why doesn't she take you back to the armpit of Canada, where you belong?" He's tried asking them where that is, exactly. Sometimes Windsor, sometimes Hamilton.

Winnipeg even, *snicker*. "You were born on the way to the hospital," his mother once told him. "Your father pulled up beside a field. I got halfway across the ditch when your head popped out." He stopped listening after that.

As with that image of his father playing on the swings with three-year-old Wolfgang. The bushy brown beard and crinkling eyes getting nearer then farther then nearer again, over and over. Each time the memory resurfaces, Wolfgang simply wills that ghostly face to keep retreating into the distance until it vanishes. It's enough to know that sometime before his fifth birthday, his father left for good.

If only it was always so easy. Lately, he's had to go out of his way to find forgetfulness, out on the snow-haunted streets. Another hit, another night, another world where everyone's on the same wavelength (until you're not). In this world, the girls don't sneer—or if they do, it's hidden behind curtains of long, limp hair. They have chipped black fingernails and smudged, crimson lips. Hardware jangles from their eyebrows, bellybuttons, and tongues. If he's lucky, they say, they'll show him their tattoo. Their arms, necks, and calves are covered with mermaids and unicorns, the entire inventory of Eden. "Not that one," they say, laughing at his firefly eyes, "Not *there*."

If there's more, Wolfgang's not sure he wants to see it.

5.

Each time he gets back, the stuff in the can at the back of the fridge looks more like cream of mushroom than chicken noodle.

"You sit down and relax," says the woman with the chicken skin. She reaches into the fridge before Wolfgang can stop her, and pulls out a can of Labatt 50.

"Here Wolfie, drink this. It'll give you some fizz."

He's not going to ask where she got that from, or how she knows his name. With any luck, she brought a six-pack.

"Visiting Montreal?" Wolfgang asks.

She's probably one of his mother's trailer park friends. The kind who sell hand-knit ponchos and read lovers' palms down by the Old Port on weekends. The kind she swore she'd never be.

"Do I look like a tourist?" says the woman. "Do I?"

"Just asking." Wolfgang holds his hands up in the air, leans back and balances on the hind legs of the bow-legged chair. So much for small talk.

"I called," she says. "I suppose you'll say your phone was dead."

Wolfgang would prefer to keep his eyes open and his wits about him, but his wits are frayed and his eyes burn with an evil itch that worsens when he rubs them. Each time he blinks, the woman's eyes change colour. A dozen different women parade in and out of the room. Their eyes are sea glass, wood pigeon, or foxfires. Their hair every shade of the visible spectrum. Their skin is as smooth as wax paper, as brittle.

"You can't sleep here," says the green-eyed, purple-dread-locked woman.

Blue bowl. Yellow chicken skin. Black gap between grey front teeth widening to an abyss.

"I'm Wolfgang," Wolfgang calls from the bottom of the abyss. "I don't think we've met."

The lips smile. A thin red lizard tongue flickers out. The chicken disappears. The bowl is a blue egg beginning to hatch.

Each one of these women has this in common: they have all been eating chicken noodle soup.

6.

Most likely, his mother had no idea how feng shui actually works. He'd come home one morning last summer to find the mirror dangling from a white thread like a poisonous spider above their front door.

"Ma!" Wolfgang yelled from the corridor. "What are you *doing?*"

His mother opened the door, a cloud of white sage smoke billowing behind her.

"Where have you been?" Her voice little girlish. She'd barely raised it above a whisper for years. Not since his father disappeared.

"What's that hanging there?" Wolfgang wasn't about to cross any threshold hexed by another of her homemade spells. Even if most of them were crock.

"You're raising your voice. Don't!"

"And you ask me why I don't come home."

"It's feng shui. From a lady at church."

He'd been to this church just once. There had been a sermon on shamanic journeying. Something about animal guides and contacting the dead. The minister talked about divine consciousness and the Spirit of life, mixing the two up as if they were interchangeable. She might as well have claimed to believe in both Jesus and Buddha.

"Feng shui," Wolfgang sighed. "So what's this mirror supposed to do, exactly?"

Whatever it was, it can't have been anything good. Soon after the appearance of the mirror came Pierre, his mother's CEGEP dropout, meat-packing-plant-worker boyfriend. Pierre spent his off-duty hours in the shower, trying to wash off the stench of death. By the end of the summer, he'd moved to a trailer in the Eastern Townships. Wolfgang's mother followed, taking most of the furniture. The dresser, the loveseat, the bookcase that sagged under the weight of bibles and almanacs. She left the bed—a futon mattress on a stack of wooden pallets—the only item Wolfgang had no use for.

Home alone at fourteen, free to come and go as long as he held down his job at the twenty-four-hour pizzeria and stayed in school. It was the first time he'd ever had his own room.

7.

This business of hair manifesting in new locations. Each erupting follicle that punctures his skin, makes him itch and scratch till his face is a raw, bleeding mess. That aching in his crotch as his balls balloon faster than his skin can stretch.

His mother would say that every ailment has its antidote, and pills don't count. Sometimes he wishes he'd nabbed her *Herb Gardener's Grimoire*. Maybe there's a few recipes in there that don't require a teaspoonful of crushed hummingbird skulls, or wild catnip harvested on the fourth quarter moon. That's why they invented pharmaceuticals. Trouble is, he's getting sloppy. Dosage, side effects, contraindications—it's hard to keep track. Doesn't help when most of the newer drugs look like rock candy or sour gummies, and seem about as potent. Used to be he could stay up all night on a bottle of NyQuil. Now he struggles to keep his eyes open even after snorting a couple ground-up tabs of Ritalin, bought off some bespectacled third grader. Wakes breathless and sweat-drenched, heart pounding. It takes him longer each time to realize he's all right, still. He's made it back to his safe place: the raft of corrugated cardboard flats pushed into the centre of the room, his homemade island, the only place he'll close his eyes.

In one year, he's grown so tall he has to fold himself into a letter Z so his feet don't touch the ground. Got to steer clear of the badlands where dust bunnies multiply, uninterrupted by human footprints.

At the murky outskirts of his domain, under the window: his mother's unmade bed. By moonlight, the sheets are pale icebergs etched with the shadows of her sleep, anointed with dust and cigarette ash.

Maybe in time he'll sleep through the night again. Get clean again. Sleep in a real bed. Just not yet.

8.

Wolfgang opens his eyes. Now the woman across the table is young and beautiful. There are green ribbons in her long red hair. He gulps down the rest of his beer and runs a hand through his own shoulder-grazing mop of streaky-dyed black. Maybe company isn't such a bad idea.

"How long are you staying?" Try not to sound too keen.

The girl smiles and her face ages by about ten years.

"You can have the bed," he adds.

Lines score the corners of her mouth, her forehead and cheeks. When she looks in the cracked bowl, her eyes turn blue. She glances back up at Wolfgang and her eyes are black again.

"Did you know," says the red-haired woman in Wolfgang's kitchen, "you used to levitate when you were a baby."

Wolfgang frowns and squeezes his empty beer can. "I don't remember."

"Floating in the darkness, fast asleep." She's braiding the ribbons into her hair. "You grew out of it by age three—about the time you started to meditate." As she teases out her long red locks, grey strands start to appear.

Wolfgang slouches lower, inside the cavernous shelter of his hoodie. It's been a hard winter. Sometimes he catches himself craving a familiar, burrowing warmth.

"What happened, Wolfie?" she says. Her face is crumpling like the can in his fist.

"What happened?" His voice sounds like those French girls, mocking.

"Where did you go?"

"Leave me alone!" Wolfgang snarls.

Grey half-moons blossom beneath her eyes.

"You were such an easy baby."

Nothing's felt easy for a long time.

"I taught you everything you know," says the white-haired crone.

Outside the window, frost feathers are drifting, dissolving into black snow. Wolfgang hurls the crushed can at the window and screams, "You're not my mother."

An aluminum star lands softly on the empty bed. Everything is quieter than the humming of the fridge.

9.

One night in a piss-stained corner beside the DJ booth, the bass so deep that Wolfgang can feel small, nameless bones in his skeleton being rearranged with each pulsing beat, he finally gets his arms around one of the girls. Pulls her, stumbling and giggling, to the mattress. Or she pushes him so that he falls and almost pokes his eye out on someone's beer bottle, someone who's already lying beneath him, whose arms reach up and drag him down. Everyone is laughing, including him. There's a pain in his right side, below his ribs. He can't remember anyone's name.

Just once, he'd like to stay awake and see what happens next, but it hasn't happened yet. These girls must go home with someone. Maybe one of these nights, it'll be Wolfgang.

10.

By age nine, he'd memorized half the contents of his mother's home library—two milk crates stuffed with second-hand occult classics. The *Gheranda Samhita* had him spellbound for years, till he discovered the *Tao Te Ching*. A flip-through of *Buckland's Complete Book of Witchcraft* left him indifferent. His Grade Four teachers marvelled as his reading level soared with no obvious effort or interest. Wolfgang himself was unimpressed. Spells and potions, mantras and rituals seemed like awfully complicated means of attaining states he'd been drifting into, mostly by accident, for as long as he could remember.

He's been trying to deprogram all conscious learning ever since. That first day, he raided the Home Depot dumpster for cardboard and foam core packaging, hauled his stash home, and secured it with a stolen roll of packing tape. Sitting cross-legged on his makeshift platform, eyes closed, the soles of his feet upturned like lotus flowers in his lap, Wolfgang learned to untether himself at will from the shores of consciousness. All evening he felt his body grow lighter, the crown of his head getting warmer, until he was surely on the verge of take-off. Always, his mother's insistent cawing ("Bedtime! Come now, there's a good boy!") pulled him back to Earth. As soon as she began to snore, he crept out from under the bedcovers and returned to his post, where he was slapped awake the next morning.

Then he turned twelve and discovered he could achieve the same results with his eyes open. As long as he wasn't lying down, there was no danger of sleep or the burden of dreams. By age thirteen, he could sustain a meditative trance for over twenty-four hours. "*Bhava samadhi,*" said his mother, in awe mixed with anxiety. She lay in bed smoking cigarette after cigarette. "You were shaking with fever but your forehead was ice."

Wolfgang had no memory of the experience or its duration. All winter he kept to himself except for those lonesome, below-zero nights when he couldn't hold out against her whimpering anymore, "My Wolfie, my baby cub."

Climbing in beside her, under the musty blankets, was the only way to make her stop.

11.

Wolfgang wakes on uncharted shores. His eyelashes are gummed with dried crud. His lips hurt when he licks them.

He forces his eyelids open, and raises his head. He's lying naked on a warm mound of tangled limbs, his torso covered with insect bites he can't scratch because he can't feel his hands. His legs are wedged under something limp and slightly damp, like beached jellyfish. He rolls to one side and the clamminess follows him; tentacles of mindless flesh cling to his. The relentless drone of drum machines and sequencers: bullets through his eardrums. The rancid odour of marinating sweat.

Wolfgang crawls to the nearest corner and vomits.

He's not the only one. All across the city, in each forsaken corner, there's a lost boy for every mother who's been up all night grasping at any spell, charm, or curse that might bring him back.

12.

He hadn't meant to lie down, hadn't wanted to risk that. Not with his mother watching from her bed, cigarette smoke unfurling in widening rings as if she herself were unravelling. Loosened by the draught from the ill-fitting window, her fine-spun, ash-blond hair wafted about her head like a fiery halo. Each time she raised her cigarette there was less of her. The ember glowed; a ring of fireflies orbited, accelerated into a vortex of golden light.

As he watched, his mother seeped right under the window sash and into the night.

13.

Wolfgang yelps as an electric current sears his eyelids and zaps the dream into oblivion.

Gradually, his eyes regain focus: a swollen, moon-like face hovers above him like a UFO. The pilot closes in on the target, the spaceship swoops down, his mother's lips suction over his.

He twists his head to one side and a viscous strand of saliva follows him, smearing itself across his cheek. "What are you *doing?*" He tastes the wetness on his lips and gags.

Wolfgang's mother sits up and pushes aside her straggling hair. A few limp strands are stuck to her forehead with sweat. Her expression is strained and slightly confused, as if she doesn't recognize him.

"What's going on?" shouts Wolfgang. "What are you doing in my bed?" He pushes her and she falls awkwardly to the floor, landing on all fours.

"Your breathing," she gasps between sobs. "You weren't breathing."

His mother kneels beside him, her head bowed, her shoulders convulsing. The sour taste of vomit lingers in his mouth. Wolfgang swallows repeatedly, and dryness sears his throat.

The last thing he remembers is the burning in his wide-open eyes.

14.

His mother used to tell him that his eyes changed colour with his mood. But each time he checked in the mirror, they were adamantly, flatly brown.

"Next time it happens, tell me, will you?" He didn't care how whiny his voice sounded. Whenever he wanted something, it felt like someone's hands were around his neck, squeezing, forcing him to beg. Anything to make her say yes.

His mother gazed through the grease-caked window at empty, stick-figure trees. "Pierre says you'll grow out of it," she said.

Pierre, with the blood of dumb animals on his hands. The summer before he left, he'd given Wolfgang a small plastic bag of dried, twig-like bits for his birthday. "What's this?" said Wolfgang, hands in his pockets. Pierre smiled, fished out one of the twigs, broke off a fingernail's worth, and put it in his mouth.

The first chance he got, Wolfgang swapped the shrooms for an acid trip. No way was he putting anything in his mouth that Pierre's hands had touched.

15.

Wolfgang finds his way home, opens the door and fumbles through a familiar darkness.

"Stay if you like," he says to the woman at the kitchen table. "I'm going to bed." He doesn't look at her. Doesn't turn the light on. Doesn't want to look through the windows of her eyes and become the thing she stares at, the thing that isn't there.

Somehow he kicks off his boots, peels sodden socks from numbed feet. The snow on his shoulders runs in rivulets to the floor. He is an island in a puddle of meltwater.

At first, he thinks that the greyish hump in the centre of the room is just a trick of the streetlight filtering in through the dirty window. How a pile of weeks-old laundry has been recast in his absence to look strangely human. Maybe he's still tripping—he left K-land hours ago. He'd check his heart rate if he could feel his fingers. No choice but to trust his eyes: the boy sitting cross-legged on the cardboard platform is no stranger. Head heavy, bent low, he could be sleeping, but Wolfgang knows he's not.

He crouches and begins to crawl across the chipped linoleum floor. He can't remember the last time he left the city, but his body remembers—did his father tell him?—this is how you trail a wild animal: belly to ground, listen, wait for it to tire. A black bear perhaps, thick skinned and crescent clawed. First, he clocks its silhouette: a shaggy, shapeless mass. Next, he fills in the bear's surroundings. It's nosing around the garbage cans outside Pierre's trailer, in a campsite at the edge of a wood. The bear gets up on its hind legs and peers in through the window; its breaths fog the glass. It sniffs its noseprints distractedly, then wanders off into the night.

Wolfgang's mother wakes and senses the bear's gaze, still lingering in the room. She holds her breath and waits for the glass to clear.

16.

Sometimes he wakes in the night, breathless and terrified that someone is watching him. Someone who was so close a moment ago, he could detect stale breath in his nostrils.

Wolfgang stretches out in his sleeping bag and feels with his toes for the known limits of his cardboard world. Then he draws his knees back into his chest and buries his head in his own warmth.

He won't venture to the edge and look over, for fear of vertigo. Besides, he already knows what he'd see, beyond the mutable map of stars and snow. The warped grid of Mile End streets with blank facades and treacherous stairs, forgotten roads that don't lead home, decoys for somewhere you have never travelled.

Above him, the darkness extends for infinite miles, eyeless
and cunning. Wolfgang listens to the creaking house, the
sleepless trees. He holds his breath so as not to wake the boy
at the centre of the dream.

Words and Colour

Nisha is going to a workshop for BIPOC writers, and Josie should come too.

What's BIPOC? Josie asks, nervously.

It sounds like a counterculture movement. Definitely alternative, possibly deviant. Something she should stay away from, the way she used to avoid hanging exclusively with the math bores and chess nerds, only to end up an outsider to pretty much every high-school clique. So far, university's just a larger pond with the same fish. She may never blend in, but she can at least try not to stick out.

Nisha doesn't ask if Josie's been living under a rock. She says, Black, Indigenous, People of Colour, like she's listing the ingredients of her favourite Booster Juice smoothie.

Am I People of Colour? Josie asks.

You're Asian Canadian.

Josie's foundation shade is Medium Ivory, just two formulas away from Nisha's Medium Taupe.

It's not about your actual skin colour, Nisha adds. It's more about having a marginalized voice because you come from a different background.

Nisha has the annoying knack of answering Josie's questions before she even asks. It's because she grew up in a large family—you learn how to read people fast.

You know I'm not a group person, Josie says.

There won't be that many people.

How do you know?

How many BIPOC writers do you know?

In all of Josie's first-year classes, white Canadians outnumber international and non-white students. If each of them was a writer, what would be the total number?

Stop trying to do the math, Nisha says. Just look at it as a way to make new friends.

I already have friends, says Josie. It's just that she can count them on one hand, whereas Nisha meets interesting people round every street corner, and talks about them as if she's known them for years. Why can't you go without me?

Because you're the only friend I have who's into this sort of thing.

But I'm not even a writer!

Yes you are—you're always writing in that notebook.

That's journalling, says Josie. It's not the same.

But Nisha won't stop there. Lots of writers write about themselves, she says. Jeanette Winterson, Rachel Cusk, Pasha Malla, Yiyun Li. People love reading that kind of stuff.

The idea of being read by other people makes Josie feel like a snail that's been poked with a stick.

Nisha says: You don't have to share your writing with the group if you're not comfortable.

Last term, there was a party at the student house Josie shares with three other medical sciences majors. She tried to avoid it by staying late at the library. Nisha found her and breathlessly explained that the guy she'd been crushing on all month had friends in the funk band that would be jamming in the backyard. Josie was the one who'd told her about the party, and she wasn't going to show up uninvited and alone.

Josie let herself be dragged home because Nisha promised not to leave her stranded—they'd be each other's moral support. With Nisha by her side, Josie wouldn't have to worry about awkward introductions. She could simply coast in the wake of already opened conversations.

Nisha's crush never showed. Sometime after midnight, she decided she was drunk enough to call him, but her phone was dead.

Josie said, Why don't you use my land line?

She put Nisha in her bedroom, and closed the door. Then she went to sit out on the front porch, where it was quieter— the stoned sociology students passing a joint around didn't seem keen on conversation. The downside was breathing in their second-hand smoke.

Half an hour later, the party showed no signs of winding down, and Josie was getting cold. She went upstairs and banged on her bedroom door, but the funk jam had moved into the living room and the beats loosening the floorboards were louder than her knuckles, so she waggled the sticky doorknob till it unlatched.

Nisha sat on the edge of Josie's bed, phone clamped between ear and shoulder. She was leafing through a spiral-bound notebook and snorting with laughter—was it at something she'd read?

As soon as she saw Josie, she flipped the book shut and slammed it down on the night stand. The receiver clattered to the floor. Josie sprang back as if repelled by an electric fence and pulled the door behind her.

Nisha came downstairs five minutes later, puppy-dog eyed. Sorry I took so long, she said.

Josie has never asked Nisha what the hell she was doing, snooping through her journal. Isn't Nisha the closest thing she has to a best friend? What could she possibly have read that Josie wouldn't willingly confide? Does it matter what Nisha—or anyone—knows or thinks about her?

On the other hand, Josie feels like she ought to put the record straight. Some days, she writes things in her notebook that she feels with every fibre of her being. The next day, she'll read her own words and wonder who that person was, with a life so vivid it must have been imagined.

Not everything in Josie's journal is true just because she wrote it.

We all need community, Nisha says. You are not an island.

Josie pictures the Toronto Islands, crowded with tourists, wedding parties, lost poets, landscape painters, nude bathers, and cyclists. You go there to get away from the city, only to find that everyone else had the same idea—we're all in the same boat.

Besides, says Nisha with a sideways glance, maybe Brian will be there.

The skin on Josie's neck starts to tingle. Soon, the redness will reach her cheeks.

I didn't know that Brian was a writer. She's not letting Nisha get away with this.

Josie's read his poems in the student magazine. She cut them out and slipped them between the eye-glazing pages of *Essentials of Clinical Geriatrics*. When the seconds slow to a torturous drip during Patient-Centred Clinical Methods: Integrated Care, she takes a discreet peek and is pulled into a timeless whirlpool. She emerges minutes later, disoriented, lost in wonder. Is it because English is the poet's second language that each word is made new?

Not everyone there will be a *writer* writer, says Nisha. It's inclusive—that's the whole point.

Inclusive, meaning including bad writers?

You're not a bad writer.

Josie looks Nisha in the eye and says, How do you know I'm not a bad writer?

There, she's said it. And it was easier than she imagined.

Up till now, she didn't think she'd ever ask. She's still not sure what kind of response she's expecting. Maybe an apology, or a confession at least.

It's fine, says Josie. You don't have to answer if you're not comfortable—

No, you're right, Nisha interrupts her. I read your note-book. I'm sorry. I shouldn't have.

And? says Josie.

I'm sorry, Nisha says again. Please don't be mad. I didn't see much, I swear—

I'm not mad, says Josie, I just want to know what you think.

Okay, says Nisha. If you really want my opinion, I think you should just ask Brian out already, instead of writing about him.

That's not what I meant, Josie says. What did you think of my writing?

I think I'd have to read it more closely, Nisha begins.

You were in my room for half an hour!

I was on the phone, says Nisha. But to be honest, your writing was way more interesting than the conversation.

So if I go to this BIPOC thing with you, Josie says, arms crossed, are you saying I'll magically fit in?

People are people, Nisha says. But it's time you found your tribe.

Josie pictures a room full of strangers brought together because they want to write. They may not know that they are writers yet, each on the verge of discovering an identity that was always theirs. What will they write about, let alone talk about? How will they find common ground?

When they look at each other, their differences will be instantly obvious. Because it is about colour after all. Colour shifts, changes, fades, merges, blooms, and shimmers like a hologram. How can she put these colours into words on a page that simply say: I am?

Legacy

The oboist and the soprano had rehearsed only twice before they found themselves on stage: a raised platform in front of an altar, in a church that relied on concerts and salsa classes to fund the maintenance of its draughty, outdated edifice.

On a small table between them, the soprano had placed a slim, crystal glass of mineral water. Beside it was the plastic vial of spittle-flecked water in which the oboist soaked her spare reeds. Often, the soprano raised her hands to her ears and fingered her diamanté cluster drop earrings. Seen from a distance, they looked real enough. Their heaviness was reassuring; the way her earlobes would ache later when she removed them.

Earlier that afternoon, the oboist had agonized between a pair of brand new, two-inch-heeled snakeskin pumps and flat-soled velvet slippers bought twenty-six years ago in Morocco. She'd backpacked across Spain after eloping with her thesis advisor at the Sorbonne. In Valencia, they fought bitterly after being robbed of their last pesetas while sleeping on La Malvarossa beach. It had been his idea to save money on hostels in favour of all-night fiestas. Luckily, their passports were stashed in the interior pocket of her windbreaker. For the rest of the trip, he kept them afloat by singing Phil Collins ballads in the streets, with a five-stringed guitar donated by a homeward-bound Briton. The velvet slippers were his last-ditch attempt to save the relationship, but she couldn't help noticing that they cost less than his engraved silver sebsi pipe, which made him look more "complacent colonialist" than *Casablanca*. Two weeks later, she was on a flight back home to Toronto—pregnant, accompanied only by the lingering scent of kief and patchouli.

At this point in the recital, after the barefoot bliss of the intermission, the oboist regretted choosing the pumps. No matter how she swayed and shifted her weight with the music's pulse, the balls of her feet found no relief. At the age of fifty-one, on the cusp of a second career, she was used to wearing only sensible shoes. She was glad about her silk-and-linen-blend pantsuit, at least. The soprano's virtually sheer, vintage Balenciaga gown was no match for the all-seeing spotlights. But perhaps that was the intended effect.

During the first rehearsal, they had briefly discussed the issue of balance.

"If you can't hear me, you're too loud," said the soprano. She'd performed Vaughan Williams's *Ten Blake Songs* more times that she cared to, and could have sung the oboe part herself.

"Everything sounds loud in here." The oboist gestured around the cell-like practice studio at the Faculty of Music, from which she'd recently graduated with a Master of Music Performance. She still felt like an imposter who might be discovered at any moment by one of her former students from the Faculty of Mathematics: *She's not an artist, she's an academic.*

The soprano put her hands over her rose-gold Swarovski bow earrings. "I can't hear myself at all," she said. In the last few months, she had noticed a recurrent ringing in her ears that lasted up to an hour after each practice session or performance.

"Maude used to say that too," the oboist observed.

The concert had been the brainchild of Professor Maude Berkeley, former high-school classmate, fellow faculty member—music not math, at the same university—and a favourite at the Vaughan Williams Society's annual chamber music series. Maude had waved aside the oboist's reservations that their respective instruments could hardly be said to complement each other—both high-pitched and prone to wailing. "Who cares what they think?" said Maude. "The main thing is that we are going to enjoy making music together, on a professional stage, where you belong."

Her aplomb had proved contagious. Whenever the oboist faltered in rehearsal during a tricky passage, she suppressed the urge to apologize. Instead, she expelled the residual air from her lungs, inhaled quickly, and launched into the next phrase before the soprano could open her mouth to complain. Ignoring the singer's beady gaze, she'd sustain an enviable legato, and end with a flourish.

"You know Professor Berkeley?" the soprano asked.

"She convinced me to devote my life to music," said the oboist. "What's left of it, anyway."

It was almost true. A two-year, unpaid sabbatical had been the least terrifying of temporary solutions. The risk to her teaching career would be minimal, and she was already a seasoned amateur.

The soprano yawned. "If we're going to do any more rehearsing," she said, "I'll need another coffee."

This was the first time the soprano had returned to Toronto since graduation, hired on short notice to replace the great Maude Berkeley, unexpectedly indisposed by stage three lung cancer and the immediate start of chemotherapy. Professor Berkeley had been her first choice for voice teacher. Instead, she'd been assigned to Dr. Gilbert Krall, an authority on liturgical music of the Franco-Flemish Renaissance. Ralph Vaughan Williams, the doyen of English modernists, was as far as he was prepared to allow her to go to fulfill the "contemporary" music requirement for her graduating recital. The jury declared that her "balance of passion and restraint" was well suited to the composer's setting of Blake's *Songs of Innocence and Experience*. That summer, Gilbert proposed to her.

She fled to New York where she quickly became something of an English music specialist, a fate she endured since it kept her calendar full without the help of that elusive middleman, the artist's agent. Over post-recital cocktails at Bar Pleiades with her piano accompanist, they routinely discussed her future.

"Give me Puccini, Verdi, Wagner even—I'm so tired of repressed emotion!"

"But you do it so well," her pianist said. He spoke with a slight lisp that made him sound French. Or perhaps that impression had something to do with his penchant for tailored gloves and engraved cufflinks.

"It doesn't pay to be an expert these days," said the soprano. "You've got to be *versatile*."

The pianist looked down at his clipped nails and buffed cuticles, and began folding his napkin into tiny accordion pleats. Before becoming a vocal coach, he'd won the Rachmaninoff Prize for Most Promising Graduate at a small but exclusive conservatory in upstate New York. The following season, he'd embarked on a concert tour of the Midwestern states. Unfortunately, audiences in Vandalia, Jacksonville, and Lorain were largely unappreciative of his programmes focusing on forgotten works by the lesser-known Romantics. If only he'd stuck with Rachmaninoff.

The soprano wondered if she'd made a faux pas by naming a notoriously anti-Semitic composer—had he also been homophobic?

"Well, maybe not Wagner," she said, finally.

"You're too sexy for Wagner," said the pianist, and smoothed the napkin over his knees. "You'd have to put on a hundred pounds to be a Valkyrie."

The soprano went home to her rented Brooklyn apartment, and wondered why the only man who understood her was both a colleague and a homosexual.

At the start of the concert, the gaunt, stern figures in the stained-glass windows had glowed brilliantly in the setting sun. Now they were invisible. Before the stage, in the vaulted darkness, were at least a hundred shadowy faces. Among them lurked the critics.

Who cares? thought the soprano, this isn't the Met. But she knew that tomorrow morning in the airport lounge, she'd scour the Arts and Entertainment section of all the major newspapers. At least her vocal cords were finally warming up. It made little difference to her, however, because when she sang, she felt as though her eardrums were being bombarded from the inside by a tuneless buzzing. All she could hear of her own voice was a muffled, underwater echo.

Since arriving in Toronto, she had kept at bay the idea that Gilbert might attend the concert. Now she shuddered to think of him out there in that faceless crowd. She recalled lessons when he'd placed his hands around her waist and massaged her abdomen, supposedly to teach her how to sing from the diaphragm. She had gasped as Gil's arms encircled her, and his hands grazed her breasts. What could she do but hold her breath?

Beside her, the oboist cast scrying circles with her instrument. The soprano was mesmerized by the oboe's gyrating bell, and the tapping toes of those awful shoes.

The oboist saw the soprano staring blankly at her and thought: *she's lost.* There was no way of cueing her, so she simply played louder.

"Soft deceit and idleness," sang the soprano, with quiet despair—then the final line of Blake's poem was drowned out by the oboe's plaint.

The oboist was shocked by the audience's rapturous applause. Had she redeemed herself in those final moments, just as the soprano was flagging?

The applause sounded tepid to the soprano, but it would be at least an hour before she could trust her ears again. She couldn't wait to return to the hotel and wash down an Extra Strength Ibuprofen with one of those miniature bottles of something or other from the minibar.

"My head's killing me," she said, and bolted toward the dressing room.

"Shouldn't we go back on stage?" said the oboist. The applause was dwindling but there was still time for a second round of bows.

"I need a cab," said the soprano. "Someone call me a cab."

The oboist noticed for the first time how similar this haughty young woman was to her own daughter, who'd always kept her at arm's length.

"We did it," she said. Pride surged within her, tempered by relief.

Sensing that a hug might be imminent, the soprano held out her hand. "Thank you," she said.

The oboist couldn't decide whether this sudden humility was a sign of genuine admiration, or plain embarrassment.

"The pleasure was mine," she said magnanimously, and grasped the soprano's hand—it was surprisingly cold. "You poor thing," she added. "You must be frozen in that dress."

The soprano managed a thin smile. She's just being protective, she told herself. Music does that to people.

Look at her shivering like a plucked chicken, thought the oboist. She made a mental note to call her daughter later. "You should have come to the concert," she imagined herself saying. "You would have loved her earrings."

The Society had prepared a modest reception of hors d'oeuvres and lukewarm white wine in plastic cups, set out on a folding table in the church basement. The oboist was the last to descend the spiral stairwell.

"Excuse me," said the treasurer, appearing suddenly round the curve of the balustrade. "I like to collect the autograph of each artist who performs for us."

He held out a copy of the programme booklet. On the cover was the image of a muscular nude, white-haired and bearded, crouched at the centre of a blazing orb. His outstretched arm was artfully positioned in front of his genitals.

"Goodness," said the oboist.

"One of Blake's most iconic paintings," said the treasurer.

"I didn't know that Blake was a painter," said the oboist, then immediately regretted it. As if her not knowing revealed a lack of rigour in her concert preparations.

"Arguably a better painter than a poet. You'd understand, being a polymath yourself." The treasurer winked.

"How did you know that?"

For a heart-stopping moment the treasurer smiled, and she felt her cheeks flush red. She hoped he'd think it was the wine.

"Programme notes," he said smugly. "It seems you've led quite the interesting life—perhaps you could add memoir writing to your list of accomplishments."

The oboist excused herself and plunged into the nearest platter of miniature sausage rolls.

Lying in bed that night, she couldn't get the image of Blake's virile, fleshly God out of her mind. If Maude had been there, she might have said, "Something for everyone," or, "You're never too old," and they would have laughed. But Maude was lying helpless in a hospital bed, despite her immortal artistry and rousing declarations. What else had she been wrong about? The oboist shivered, recalling that brooding frown on the treasurer's still-handsome face. It might have been the result of a stroke, but there was no other evidence to support that theory.

I'm in my fifties, she thought, and I've never been in love.

At the next meeting of the Vaughan Williams Society, the agenda included:
The need for a new concert venue.
The expense of hiring out-of-town soloists.
A marked decrease in membership, proportional to the rise in median age of the remaining trustees.

The treasurer said that featuring more performers whom young people could identify with ought to bring in the next generation of classical music enthusiasts.

"That soprano fit the bill nicely," someone said.

"The oboist poured her heart and soul into it," the chairwoman said quickly. "She was practically dancing."

"She certainly was," said the treasurer. He leaned back and crossed his arms. "But is that enough?"

"Talent, dedication, and maturity of artistic expression," said the chairwoman. "Is there something I'm missing?" She was the Society's only female member since the treasurer's wife passed away the previous year.

"I'm sure she's a wonderful woman," said the treasurer. "But why not invest in up-and-coming students—young musicians who'll carry our torch for decades to come? That'll keep costs down."

"I think we should table this discussion for the time being and come back with more concrete suggestions next time," said the chairwoman. "Unless anyone has constructive comments about the concert."

"I don't think those were our Ralph's best works," someone said hesitantly.

"Perhaps not," said the chairwoman. "But we are the guardians of his legacy, not his judge."

Vintage Chanel and a Paper Fan

Toronto in July, and the air is as thick and soupy as Hong Kong in August. Connie's been at the bus stop for ten minutes, in her Gucci sunglasses and straw fedora, and already she can feel sweat soaking the underarms of her linen tunic with the mandarin collar.

Every Saturday for the past two years, Connie and her best friend Mary have met for dim sum lunch at their favourite Chinatown restaurant. Today, Mary is bringing a friend she'd like her to meet. Gordon is a professor of anthropology, specializing in East Asian studies. Perhaps Connie could help Gordon with his research?

After living in Canada for thirty years, Connie's sure that Gordon knows more about East Asia than she does, but Mary's having none of it. Connie speaks the language, she says, it's in her blood.

Connie has repeatedly assured Mary that her Cantonese is at least as good as Connie's English. But Mary's too embarrassed to practise speaking it. In any case, she demurs, she can't read Chinese characters.

When Connie arrives at the restaurant, she looks for her friend at their regular table for two, but of course she's not there. Mary's seated at a larger table, beside a white-haired, English-looking man. She waves Connie over, and the man rises and places his hands together at his heart.

Lei hou, he says to Connie, with a bow. Unfortunately, that's about the extent of my Cantonese.

Nice to meet you, Connie says in English.

There are two empty chairs at the table. Connie parks her purse on the one beside Gordon.

I love your purse, says Mary. Is it vintage Chanel?

This old thing? says Connie. I've had it forever.

Time was when Connie would buy a new model every season. Before they emigrated, her husband had been a high-flying executive, which pitted Connie in direct competition with the other executives' wives. Over five-course business dinners, they brandished logo-emblazoned accessories. The gaudier the better. Chanel's classic quilted caviar leather bag, with gold chain strap and double-C clasp, was Connie's pièce de résistance.

Inside the purse: red *lai-seeh* envelopes, packets of Kleenex, a Gucci wallet almost as big as the purse, chrysanthemum cough drops, and a folded paper fan. Painted on the fan: a Chinese watercolour landscape, and a few lines of calligraphy. Connie rummages through her purse and produces the fan triumphantly. She flicks it open in one swift, practiced motion.

What a great idea, says Gordon.

I should have brought mine, says Mary.

My goodness, says Gordon, peering at the tiny, stylized brushstrokes. Is that a Wang Wei poem?

The fan had belonged to Connie's grandmother. The old woman would sit all day on her balcony in a wicker chair, surrounded by potted plants. Their lush leaves and engorged blooms feasted on the tropical humidity. After school, before her parents came home for dinner, Connie fanned her grandmother while she napped. If the fanning stopped, the old woman's eyelids snapped open, and the clouded eyes grew piercing.

Good for nothing girl, are you sleeping on the job?

No, Grandmother.

Connie would resume her task hurriedly, before the fan could be snatched away.

A folded fan left a different kind of bruise than the feather duster, the leather belt, or the ruler. The last two were reserved for Connie's older brothers. But their skin was thicker.

I wish I could read Chinese, Mary is saying. She turns to Gordon: How long did it take you to learn?

I thought you didn't know much Cantonese, Connie says.

Gordon's fluent in Mandarin, says Mary. He used to teach at Yangcheng University.

Luckily, the written forms of both languages are almost identical, Gordon says. He is still squinting at the fan.

It belonged to my grandmother, Connie says.

It looks like an antique, says Gordon. May I?

He takes the fan with both hands and a slight bow. She considers pointing out that no one bows in Hong Kong—she'd been struck by the difference in etiquette when accompanying her husband on business trips to South Korea and Japan—but Mary is beaming, so she bites her tongue.

Gordon studies the fan so closely that she half expects him to pull out a magnifying glass.

All those exiled poets of the Tang dynasty, he says. They were foreshadowing the Cultural Revolution by thirteen hundred years.

Why don't you read the poem out loud to us? says Connie. We wouldn't know if you were faking it.

Oh I'm sure you would, says Gordon.

Connie's just being modest, says Mary, and darts her a warning look as the waitress arrives with their order.

Three is the perfect number for sharing dim sum. Most items are bite-sized, and served as a trio. Three char siu buns. Three spring rolls. Three deep-fried taro root dumplings. Gordon says he's never tasted better Chinese food outside China.

What about food in Hong Kong? says Connie.

Gordon looks confused.

Connie doesn't consider Hong Kong to be part of China, Mary explains.

Love for one's homeland, says Gordon, and nods. Very Chinese.

Then four shrimp dumplings arrive in a bamboo steamer. By the end of the meal, the fourth dumpling is still untouched.

Do you want the last one? says Mary.

You can have it, says Connie.

Gordon?

I'm staying out of this, says Gordon.

For God's sake, says Connie.

She waves the waitress over, and asks her to cut the dumpling into three equal portions. The girl stares at Connie as if this might be a practical joke.

It's already tiny, says Mary. You're crazy.

It makes perfect sense, says Connie. Since we're all too polite.

The girl gets to work with a pair of stainless-steel scissors. Twice, the shrimp inside the rice-flour wrapper escapes the snapping blades, but is finally severed. The miniature portions are too small to be eaten with chopsticks, so Connie impales them on wooden toothpicks.

Forgive my fingers, says Gordon.

It's a traditional Hong Kong custom, says Connie, straight-faced. We don't believe in wasting even the last grain of rice.

How egalitarian, says Gordon. He folds his napkin carefully, and excuses himself for the washroom.

What is wrong with you? says Mary, once Gordon is out of sight.

What's wrong with me? says Connie. Don't you think he's a little pretentious?

He's a professor! And he loves Chinese culture.

His version of Chinese culture. Not mine.

I know I wasn't born there, Mary sighs, but Hong Kong was part of China way before it was a British colony.

I don't even have a Hong Kong Identity Card anymore, says Connie.

She thinks of Grandmother beating her grandchildren solemnly, one after another. Always for their own good.

One day you'll thank me, Grandmother had said.

The day Connie and her husband left Hong Kong, there were at least two dozen relatives at the airport to see them off. The smell of Tiger Balm. Flash bulbs going off. Fistfuls of Kleenex.

I have something for you, said Grandmother.

Connie flinched when the fan was placed in her hand.

May it bring you good luck in Canada.

Connie can't remember if she said thank you for the gift, never mind the blessing.

From across the crowded dining hall, Gordon approaches, weaving his way carefully between the closely packed tables. His progress is impeded by his insistence on stepping politely aside for each waiter and pushcart that crosses his path.

Every year I feel less and less Chinese, says Connie. Especially since Eddie died.

That's why I thought you'd like to meet Gordon.

Why don't you date him, since you like him so much?

His ex-wife was from Fujian, Mary begins, then falls quiet as Gordon arrives at their table.

Connie knows what Mary was about to say: *I couldn't compete with a real Chinese.*

When the bill arrives, Mary reaches for it. Connie slaps her hand away.

Let me pay, says Mary. Lunch was my idea.

What are you talking about? says Connie. We do this every weekend.

If you'll allow me, says Gordon, it would be my pleasure.

You're the guest, says Mary.

Please, says Gordon, I insist.

Thank you, Gordon, says Mary. You'll have to let us return the favour sometime.

Connie slides the fan across the table.

A gift for our honoured guest, she says. Mary's crazy if she thinks she'll consent to another meeting with Gordon.

Oh I couldn't, says Gordon. It's a family heirloom.

Mary smirks and says, You could return it to Connie next time.

Well now, says Gordon. That's an idea.

I don't need it back, Connie says quickly. I have several at home.

You don't know what this means to me, says Gordon. I'm a huge Wang Wei fan.

He opens the fan and reads in Mandarin: "All alone in a foreign land / I am twice as homesick on this day."

Wow, says Mary. That was beautiful. What does it mean?

Those Tang dynasty poets certainly knew how to write about loneliness, says Gordon.

The poet *thinks* he'd be less homesick if he wasn't alone, says Connie. But homesickness isn't something you can cure.

Nowadays, most of us can get on a plane and go home whenever we want—but what if it doesn't feel like home anymore? Maybe it's better to feel homesick than to find out that the place you came from no longer exists.

Perhaps, says Gordon, the poet is saying he'd rather be homesick than alone.

Connie is silent. She's had thirty years to reflect on the meaning of that stanza, and she's never read it as a love poem.

Coming to Canada has taught her that the past only has power over you as far as you look back. She's applied the same principle to Eddie, donating his belongings and renovating the condo within two weeks after his funeral. They never used to talk much anyway. He had his golf buddies, she had her luncheons. So why are tears springing to her eyes now, for the first time in two years?

Are you all right? says Mary.

I'm fine.

Thank heaven Gordon hasn't noticed. He's smiling at the waitress who has just returned with the credit card machine, and waving his American Express vaguely above it as if he's never seen one of these contraptions before.

To him, the world of the poem is a tapestry of ideas—subtle, intricate, intoxicating even, worthy of a lifetime's study—but ultimately foreign.

How was everything? the waitress asks.

It was wonderful, says Gordon. Poetry and fine dining with two lovely ladies; what more could I ask for?

The following Saturday, Mary waits for Connie at their usual table.

No Gordon today? says Connie, and clutches her heart in mock despair.

I don't know why you have to be so mean, says Mary. He's nice. And he likes you.

I don't want a man, no thank you, says Connie. I like my freedom.

Why can't you give him a chance?

I gave him my fan, says Connie. Do you know how hot my bus ride home was?

I can't believe you gave away your grandmother's fan.

Are you serious? says Connie. Do you really think I would give a priceless antique to someone I just met?

You mean it's not your grandmother's fan?

Of course not! The original is almost 100 years old.

But it looked so ... authentic.

It's meant to. It's a replica.

You had an exact copy made?

Connie nods. Two, in fact.

Why? Mary looks truly baffled.

Before last week Connie might have said that, while she's never been one for sitting around and moping, you need to honour your roots. But how to explain her reasons for curating a past she can live with? Her abiding dread of that long-dead matriarch hardly matters—it's her fan now. A key to a world of living memory, hidden in a bedside drawer alongside carved jade miniatures, a few pieces of porcelain, and Eddie's favourite cufflinks. The fan stirs the drowsy heat of a Toronto summer, and the breeze is tinged with a faint odour of mothballs and camphor. Connie smiles, closing her eyes, as ripples of cool air erase the pink, smarting weal across a pigtailed schoolgirl's trembling palm.

Nostalgia's a funny thing, she says out loud.

Mary sighs. I wonder when Gordon will realize he's been given a fake.

That reminds me. Connie reaches under her chair, and places a large Holt Renfrew gift bag on the table.

What's this? says Mary.

Look inside.

Mary's face becomes even more incredulous. You're giving this to me?

No need to get too excited, says Connie. It's not like I went out and bought it.

But it's yours, says Mary. Are you sure you don't want it?

She reaches into the gift bag and pulls out the quilted Chanel purse. Its scuffed corners have been smoothed and polished, and apart from a few creases in the leather, it looks almost new.

I took it to this shoe repair place, says Connie. I think they did a good job.

It's gorgeous, says Mary. If you ever want it back, just let me know.

I don't need it, says Connie. I got a new one—from Roots. She holds up a brand new crossbody, in orange-hued leather.

Ooh, very fashionable, says Mary, absently. She's still mesmerized by the Chanel purse.

What if it's not a real Chanel? Connie teases. Do you still want it?

That's not the point, says Mary. It's special because it's yours.

That's why I wanted you to have it.

Oh Connie, says Mary. She looks like she might cry.

How many years have we known each other? Connie asks.

Mary thinks for a minute. What year did you come to Canada?

It doesn't matter, says Connie. Let's just say it's been forever. That's how it feels, anyway.

Night Watch

The woman sitting in the dark, on the front porch of the house with the immaculate lawn and crab-apple tree, is on her phone again. He hears the staticky jumble of alien speak when he walks past. The woman herself stays silent.

This has been going on for a week. His evening routine has been unsettled by the appearance of this woman, whom he has never seen before.

The walk was supposed to help with his insomnia, which worsened after he moved to the city for his job. When he retires, he will live on top of a mountain, with only goats and vultures for company. For now, this leafy, middle-class neighbourhood, which boasts a large park with a hiking trail and an off-leash dog area, is the closest he can get to living in nature. He is allergic to dogs.

If he had a dog, he'd feel better about walking through the park at night, alone. Is this what his therapist intended? A dark shadow moving across the unlit soccer field. Dangerous.

Does this woman think him dangerous? Her house is at the end of the cul-de-sac, out of reach of the cone of light spreading from the last streetlamp, where the road refuses to go further, like a spooked horse turning tail before the park begins. Beyond is a deep, fiery darkness, alive with fireflies and the blue-white flash of cottontail rabbits streaking through the undergrowth, beneath the bellyful keening of coyotes.

He slows his pace when approaching the park, till he has stopped outside the last house. He turns his head to glance up through the shadows of the crabapple tree branches at the figure seated on the porch, and strains to catch a sentence, a word. A single clue that might help him enter this woman's silence.

She shows no sign of having noticed him.

The voice on the other end of her phone spills out into the faceless night, in a thousand unintelligible fragments. To whom does it belong? An absent partner? An anxious friend? An ex-lover threatening to kill himself again?

Her silence suggests that whatever the reason for the call, there's time enough to answer. Each night, her silence snowballs. Her patience is unfathomable.

Once inside the park, he pounds the circular trail with long, firm strides, glancing over his shoulder occasionally in spite of himself until he has exited again, with nothing in his mind but haste to reach the safety of light. His heart rate does not decrease till he reaches his own, well-lit street. Only then does he think of the woman on the phone.

Later, lying awake in the dark, he wonders if she is still outside her house. Whether her one-sided conversation has resolved. He fights the urge to get out of bed, slip on his sneakers, and find out. By now the porch must be empty, the windows darkened, the woman asleep.

He closes his eyes and tries to count backwards from one hundred, but he already knows it won't work. As a last resort, he tries the visualization exercise his therapist taught him, though he's never successfully completed it.

First, he pictures a black box with an old-fashioned lock—not his digital home safe, whose password he keeps forgetting. He is to envision the box floating in space, in a lightless vacuum, free from all distractions. Into this box he must place every last thought, care, and worry.

Except tonight, he sees himself carrying the box under his arm as he walks briskly toward the park. He approaches the house at the end of the cul-de-sac, and heads calmly up the garden path.

The woman barely has time to register his approach: a strange man in a hooded sweatshirt with a dark object under one arm. She screams, and the person she was listening to stops in mid-sentence, shocked by her interjection.

There is a momentary silence in which she sees her possible futures. They are all infinitely more horrible than anything she's ever been told, however painstakingly described to her in excruciating detail.

In the split second of registering that this man is bearing down on her, extending one hand as if to grab her or her phone, she sees her own rape and violent death.

But this does not happen.

The man hesitates, as if bewildered by her reaction. He takes a step back and says, Sorry if I frightened you, it's just that your phone has been keeping me awake all week.

She notices that he can't be much older than her, although his face is lined and weary.

What's that? she says weakly, indicating the box under his arm.

My therapist told me to put in here everything I can't let go of.

The woman is still afraid, but the tiniest glimmer of hope has appeared. In her apprehension, she begins to understand that by speaking with him, she is buying time.

She says: What will you do with the box afterwards?

I don't know.

His therapist told him to picture himself locking it and throwing away the key, far away into the universe, never to be found. He looks up at the sky and its blackness seems impenetrable, its coldness inhuman.

If I were you, says the woman, I'd leave your box under a tree in the park.

The man shivers at the thought of that prowling darkness.

She must have noticed his discomfort, because she says, If you're afraid, I'll walk with you.

He looks at her askance. How can he trust her? A stranger, though they are nearly neighbours.

She stands up slowly, placing her phone deliberately on her empty seat as if to say that wherever they are going now, there is no need for conversation.

Trust me, she says, I know my way around.

The man lets himself be guided back down the garden path. The woman stays close by his shoulder, steering him with her voice.

This way, she murmurs. A little to the left, now straight ahead. Mind your step. Watch out for that low-hanging branch.

Somewhere behind them, in a distant past, her phone resumes its litany to the starless night. A broken chant:

Hello, can you hear me? Are you there? Say something. Speak to me. What's going on? Please tell me what's going on.

Visions of Sophia

I t's not the first time Sophie's seen the busker on the boardwalk, in his pale blue denim suit and sombrero. He's been outside the Italian restaurant's umbrella-shaded patio most days this summer, which makes him pretty much unavoidable.

Sophie and Marty's lakeside condo is right next to a pedestrian mall, just a few steps east along the boardwalk. Marty bought their unit in the late eighties, when they were newlyweds, long before condo living was hip. Eighth floor, window wall, panoramic view of Lake Ontario. It's proved a sound investment.

When Sophie goes grocery shopping, she walks out through the revolving glass doors, turns left down the board-walk, and left again after the Italian restaurant, to enter the mall.

This is how she knows that Sombrero only performs Bob Dylan covers, complete with guitar and foot tambourine. Sometimes he gets the lyrics mixed up, invoking leopard-skin-pill-box-hat-wearing tambourine players to the tune of "Visions of Johanna". Sophie's never sure if he's really forgotten the words or just trying to see if anyone's paying attention, snarling at homeward-bound nine-to-fivers hurrying past, busy on their smartphones.

He delivers these mashed-up, sneering diatribes in a growly baritone instead of Dylan's nasal tenor. An improvement on

the original, Sophie has to admit, but she's always been more
of a Simon and Garfunkel kind of girl.

In her first year at university, she dated a jazz saxophon-
ist who gave her a mix tape of that year's hits, including
"I'm Not in Love," and "Fifty Ways to Leave Your Lover." She
was a shy classical music major, newly arrived in Canada.
Her sole exposure to popular music had been her mother's
Cantopop addiction. The previous year's Sam Hui album,
Games Gamblers Play, was the pinnacle of cool.

Two weeks later the saxophone player moved to New York.
Sophie threw out the mix tape along with a chewed-up reed
he'd given her as a souvenir. The experience left her with a
lifelong dislike of jazz, but she had to admit that the folk–pop
ballad by the two Jewish boys was a pretty good song. Until
she met Marty when she was twenty-two, the duo's easygoing,
companionable warbling provided consolation during more
than one breakup.

She was surprised to learn that they'd spent their entire
career clawing at each other's throats.

On days when she can't handle another rendition of "Just
Like a Woman," Sophie takes the long way round to the
mall's street-facing entrance. But if she's pressed for time,
she'll quicken her steps, stiffen her shoulders, and give the
busker as wide a berth as possible. Caught in a bottleneck,
she'll half turn to him and shake her head slightly, as if to
say: Sorry, no change today.

Not that he's ever given her a response. He just keeps playing, a slight smile on his sunburned face, his eyes half-closed
as if in ecstatic communion with the god of guitarists. As if
he's above mundane concerns.

Perhaps he's not doing it for the money.

Sophie's seen buskers pack up after a day's work and drive away in gleaming SUVs. She once read that the violinist Joshua Bell had busked, incognito, in Washington D.C.'s Union Station, and no one stopped to listen. What did he expect, with classical music?

Even if you manage to make a living, the pay will never compensate for a lost childhood spent indoors, practising your instrument. Before she left home, she hadn't realized there was a difference between Sam Hui's profession and the one her parents signed her up for. She'd started studying the piano at age six. Her world grew narrower.

Sombrero's probably never had a music lesson in his life. Not that she can tell by his playing—she's never actually stopped to listen. Who does, apart from tourists?

Music's always in the background to city life, disposable, forgettable. You get used to tuning out the noise. These days, Sophie's Spotify playlist is an anonymous potpourri of ambient soundscapes—Tibetan flutes, running water, synthetic harmonies with vaguely angelic overtones. They're meant to help her relax, sleep better, lower her blood pressure, improve her memory.

She'd stopped playing long ago. Long before her last student quit. When did she last sit down and listen to music for its own sake?

Today, she's slipped out to grab a bottle of white for dinner while the lemon cod's in the oven. Marty usually picks up some red on his way home, but that won't work with cod, and there's no point texting him. He's probably in a meeting and by the time he gets out, he'll have forgotten.

Standing in the rush-hour line-up for the single available checkout, she realizes that the chorus of "Like a Rolling Stone" is stuck in her head like a feedback loop. To be without a home. To have to get used to it. Was that what Sombrero was playing five minutes ago, when she passed by?

She can't remember. She must have screened it out along with the rest of the city's voices. The only thing she's sure of is that she's never learned the lyrics to this song. So how come every word is echoing in her head right now like a three a.m. smoke alarm?

It strikes her for the first time that the poetry's surprisingly profound. As if there might actually be some genuine pain and hard-won humility beneath the grating voice and indifferent cool. Has she been underestimating Dylan for all these years?

When she comes out of the mall the busker is alone. He must be tuning his guitar in between songs. But no, he's simply strumming the same chord quietly, over and over. Sophie lingers, lulled by the rhythmic drone. Either he's having a memory lapse, or he hasn't decided what to play next.

What's the root of that chord?

Once she had a superpower. She could pluck notes out of the air and name them. Her teachers called it "perfect pitch". But after forty, the magic leaves you. Notes you used to know by name, perfectly arrayed in chromatic constellations, start to become strangers.

She's been caught out. Why didn't she have the presence of mind to keep on walking? Sombrero's heavy-lidded eyes are wide open, looking straight at her. He gives her a nod and an almost imperceptible smirk, as if he knows her. As if he knows she has no intention of giving him money. As if he understands her perfectly, and has forgiven her.

Sophie stands there, not three feet from this man, clutching the bottle of wine with both hands. She now wishes she'd paid the extra for a plastic bag. Maybe he thinks she's an alcoholic. A middle-aged, Asian woman slightly the worse for drink. An easy mark.

But no, these are not the eyes of a man who would cause her harm. They are an unearthly grey; not bluish or hazel but truly monochromatic, and soft as down. She wants to lose herself in their airy depth. To feel herself falling upwards through a pale, endless sky.

But she must stay alert. There is something she must attend to. These eyes have an important message for her. They tell her that she, Sophia Richards née Chan, and this man have met hundreds of times before, in different places, in different lives.

Each time, they've had to pretend that they're strangers. Driven to play out this charade for the benefit of other people; for the millions who will never understand what it is they share. A language without words, instantly understood, faster than you can recall the title of a song.

The last chord sounds. The busker doffs his sombrero and salutes his audience of one.

I'm taking requests, he says. What's your fancy?

Sophie looks round. All she sees are shoppers strolling by, unheeding. None of them seem interested in Bob Dylan covers. He must be speaking to her, yet what did he mean? It must be part of the charade.

Let me guess, he says with a gap-toothed smile, you're a Simon and Garfunkel fan.

Sophie catches her breath and gulps. A silver hook slips down her throat. It's all she can do not to drop the wine bottle.

How did you know?

Just a feeling, he says, and starts strumming the intro to "Mrs. Robinson."

His features start to blur. Sophie blinks, and reaches a hand toward her face. What's the matter with her eyes? Here are her glasses, resting on her nose, where they always are. What's this wetness on her cheek?

I'm sorry, she mumbles, I have to go. She can't let him see her like this, even though he's seen her soul. She turns away, head down, and merges with the crowd.

You're gorgeous, lady!

In any other instance, that would have been a warning, a prelude to a pass. But not the way he says it. Gentle, lilting, in his normal speaking voice, which she realizes she's never heard before. It's surprisingly light, compared to the gravely baritone of his singing.

So light, she can't be sure she heard him right.

Sophie stops in her tracks. A man behind her grumbles, sidestepping. But there's no time to worry about that. She turns back, against the current of the crowd, toward the sound of the guitar.

Did he really say that?

Bleary-eyed, she swims back, drawn by that unmistakeable opening riff, those syncopated chords with the twanging low G, or is it an F-sharp? Here comes the first verse and she could have sworn he just changed the words.

… *Mrs. Richardson* …

She reaches him too late. That half-smile lifting the muscles around his cheekbones, his eyelids at half mast, tell her that he's no longer here, outside this restaurant patio at the end of August. He's in that private place where she was too, just moments ago. That state which makes everyone on the outside a mere spectator. Faceless. Voiceless. Unknowable.

Somehow, despite feeling as though she's walking along the bottom of the lake, Sophie makes it home. She puts the wine in the freezer and wishes she could crawl in there with it. Her heart hasn't stopped racing since she got in, and she's worried it will trigger another hot flash. She thought she was done with all that five years ago. But her body continues to remind her it has a life of its own that no amount of medication can control.

At least her head has cleared enough for her to make some sense of what just happened out there on the boardwalk. *Newsflash: Postmenopausal Asian Engulfed by Troubled Waters.* Maybe she should check her temperature.

But first, better get the cod out of the oven.

She's grappling with the cast iron casserole when Marty calls, and almost burns herself when the phone buzzes to life. Its vibrations propel it across the counter like a fish flapping on the deck. She lets it go to voicemail, but Marty doesn't leave a message and calls right back. By now, she's taken off her oven mitts but still doesn't pick up.

She leans against the kitchen counter, grips the counter's bevelled, granite edge with both hands, and waits for the phone to stop vibrating. The granite is slippery with oil or water. Or maybe it's her sweating palms.

A text message pops up. He's held up on a conference call with some folks in China who're still trickling in from breakfast. He'll be another hour at least.

She wipes down the counter, and texts back: *Fish for dinner. You might want to pick up some white.*

Twenty minutes later, she's out of the shower, spritzing herself with *L'Air du Temps*, prepping her face with retinol moisturizer so her foundation won't crack later.

She puts on a clean shirt and a slimmer pair of slacks, then realizes it'll be too obvious that she's made an effort. Nothing for it but to change back into the clothes she's been cooking in, and hope they don't reek of cod. She's only been wearing them for a couple of hours anyway. Lately, her mornings have ground to a halt, and she barely makes it out of pyjamas till after lunch.

Marty had been wary when she stopped the Zoloft at the beginning of June. He remembered what happened when she'd tried to quit last time, and the time before. She's promised she'll talk to her doctor, but what's she going to prescribe? Another meditation CD?

Music though can capsize your life in an instant. It can suck you in and under in the blink of an eye.

Sophie realizes she's been humming under her breath since she got back in the elevator with a bottle cooler, olive jar, cream crackers, and a couple of clear plastic tumblers inside a Vera Bradley tote. What's the name of that tune again? Why can't she think of the words? They were right inside her head earlier, like bees in a hive. Whatever the song's called, it's in her blood now like that half glass she downed after popping the cork.

She'd been on her way out when she remembered the corkscrew. As she stood there, holding the condo door with one hand, the tote bag in the other, the elevator had slid open and one of the neighbours, a woman with a yapping Pomeranian who'd moved in earlier this year, had stuck her head out and called down the hallway: Are you coming?

She'd bolted back inside the apartment, hoping the woman would assume she simply hadn't heard. Another split-second decision: opening the bottle right then and there in the kitchen. What else was she supposed to do? Bring the corkscrew with her? Perhaps she ought to leave the olives behind too.

She taps her toes as the floors spool down to zero, a counter rhythm to the tune she's humming. She shouldn't have had wine on an empty stomach. Blame it on the music. This is all a bit crazy, but when was the last time she had fun? Don't think this through or you'll talk yourself out of it. Take a deep breath, and jump.

What's he going to be playing when she gets there? Cynical Bob or soulful Paul?

Outside the Italian restaurant there's no sign of the busker. Sophie scans the boardwalk for a sombrero in the sea of baseball caps and Tilley hats. Maybe he went to use the washroom. Maybe he's gone to have a smoke.

The sun's going down, and Sophie shivers. She should have brought a shawl. She'd thought of the shawl earlier, in the shower, and how nice it would be to lay it out like a picnic blanket. But then there had been the need to change outfits, and the brief struggle with the corkscrew.

She sits down on a bench, feeling conspicuous among the kissing couples and families with small children. A group of skateboarders come scraping past, whooping it up. One of them screeches to a halt in front of Sophie and says, Hey lady, need help finishing that? He's eyeing the wine bottle, poking out of the tote bag.

Sophie recoils. He can't be much older than fourteen.

The boy flips his skateboard around. You need to take a chill pill, he shouts over his shoulder as he glides off.

Sophie gets to her feet. The condo is only a block away, but her teeth are chattering and she's starting to shake. It's the damn bottle, ice cold, condensation soaking her thin silk shirt. She could just leave it here and make some homeless wino's day. But the toddler of a family seated to her right is peering at her, with that wide-eyed scrutiny that toddlers have.

Sophie forces a smile at the child, and he bursts into tears.

She starts walking, away from the condo, unsure of where she's going. The night is young. It's not too late to turn this around. She just needs to move, get her blood pumping. Once the body warms up, it'll tell her what it needs; where to go.

Behind her, someone calls out, Hey lady, hey!

She doesn't recognize the voice and has no idea if it's addressing her, but instinctively, she half turns to see where it's coming from.

Stay, lady, stay!

This time, she notices a sharpness to the voice, a mocking edge. She hurries onward. Keep walking, don't look back, don't let them scare you. Back straight, poker face. Follow the crowd. Why are there so many people out tonight? Why shouldn't there be? It's downtown Toronto; you could lose yourself and never be found.

And then, ahead, the sound of a guitar. Someone singing. Sophie hurries forward, her heart in her mouth, and stops at the edge of a small crowd. In the middle of the semicircle, a young black man in dark glasses holds a microphone in one hand, its black cord uncoiling from a boom box as he belts out "Amazing Grace" in a bright, clear tenor. In his other hand, he carries a white cane.

Sophie can't take her eyes off him. He holds her attention the way he holds that of every single person standing before him, in the spell of his song. Their silence suggests that, in each of their minds, they are no longer outside on a windy boardwalk between Lake Ontario and a busy highway but inside the lush velvet majesty of the Elgin Theatre or Massey Hall.

He finishes with a falsetto flourish, and his audience whoops and applauds. Then he plucks the white fedora from his head, turns it upside down and proffers it, slowly panning toward the sound of applause, the words of praise. Those who stood near the back during his performance come forward, eager to make themselves known.

Thank you sir, God bless, he murmurs. Thank you ma'am, that's very kind of you. The crowd is thinning but Sophie stays where she is, unable to look away, till there's no one left standing between them. He's about fifteen feet away, his back to the blue-black lake. His head is turned in her direction and for a heart-stopping instant she feels as though he is staring straight at her. But he can't be.

Sorry, she says, raising her voice to be sure he hears her. I left my wallet at home.

He takes a few hesitant steps in her direction, tapping with his cane. She looks into the black lenses, stricken.

Here. She comes closer, holding the bottle of wine at arm's length. Do you want this? It's all I've got.

The young man doesn't move.

Take it. Take the whole thing.

He's blind, lady, someone says. He doesn't know what you're talking about.

Why does she feel so certain he can see her?

It's all I've got, she says, firmly. Do you want it or not?

The singer turns away. He begins to gather up his microphone cord, looping it carefully in perfect, concentric circles, gauging the length of the cord with his hands.

Just take it, Sophie says, louder now. I know you want it. I don't need it. I can't bring it back home. Just take it away, please. Somebody, take it away.

Suddenly, there's a hand on her shoulder.

Are you all right, ma'am? Someone's come up behind her and is talking to her in a low, soothing voice, as if to a frightened animal.

Are you lost? Do you need help?

Sophie turns toward this warm, dark, comforting voice, but she doesn't dare look up at the stranger's face. She nods silently.

Are you okay? Do you want me to call an ambulance?

No ambulance, Sophie says. I just want to go home.

All right, we'll get you home. Where do you live?

She raises her arm to point, but when she looks around, all she sees is darkness, peppered with an ever-moving display of lights that only confuse her further. Passing traffic, streetlights changing, the sudden glare from a swerving bicycle's headlamp, a blinding flash from a nearby camera.

Do you know where you live? says her patient interrogator. If you don't know, I can try to get help for you.

Sophie wonders what kind of help they have in mind. What would Marty think if she ended up in the hospital? Probably that he'd been right all along.

I'm not sure what happened, she says carefully, but I've lost my bearings. I was out for a walk, and now I'm lost. It's never happened to me before. I'll be all right. I just need a moment to find myself, then I'll be all right.

The Truth About Aging

I found my first grey hair at twenty-seven. That year I pulled out at least a dozen, staring in the mirror in my boyfriend's basement bedroom at his parents' house.

My boyfriend was a jazz drummer, and jazz jams usually start around midnight. Most mornings, I crawled back to the basement alone while he was still crushing caffeinated renditions of Cole Porter ballads.

One afternoon, we woke to drops of cold water splashing onto our faces. The ground-floor toilet tank had cracked and flooded after his father over-tightened the mounting bolts. Years of band practice in the studio below had shaken the screws loose, and the tank had started to detach from the toilet bowl.

If my boyfriend wasn't a drummer, we wouldn't have been rudely awakened by waste water.

For six months after the breakup, I scoured my scalp daily for signs of grey among the black. I found nothing.

Since my twenty-eighth year, discipline and self-control have kept my hair growing on the right side of thirty. Mistakes are unavoidable, and at times the enemy takes root. Years can go by without incident, when out of the blue I'll spot a silver sprout, or arctic pube. When that happens, I remind myself I'm only human. Then I reach for my tweezers.

Sometimes, a closer look reveals that the hair has changed its mind and gone back to growing in black. I leave it in as a warning against a life of monthly Subscribe & Save Clairol deliveries.

Then there are the red, blonde, and copper strands whose origins are a mystery—a change in diet, hormones, or Mongolian ancestors, perhaps. I don't infringe on their colourful diversity. They're my lucky streaks.

My brush with greying has taught me to make the most of however long I've got. My mane may never rival Rapunzel's, but she had an early start (stolen at birth, locked in a tower). I wear mine in a fishtail braid wound thrice round my waist like a girdle, or as a neck warmer. Some days I go the extra mile and build a beehive pompadour worthy of Marie Antoinette's head.

I'm fifty-five years old, and my hair has never looked younger. Full and dark as a Groenendael's coat, with artful highlights. People stop me in the street and ask for the secret to my natural-looking colour. Your hair looks so healthy, they exclaim. I know what they mean: *for your age*. I just smile enigmatically, Mona Lisa style, to avoid deepening those laugh lines.

It's been more than twenty-seven years since I woke with sewage on my face, but you can't be too careful. I rise early and go to bed before midnight. I avoid basements, and check the plumbing before I flush. If jazz comes on the radio, I switch channels. I've risked less than a handful of dates—and regretted them the next morning as soon as I peered in the mirror, comb in one hand, magnifying glass in the other. I'd rather stay in and wash my hair.

This year, I bought my first home: a thirty-ninth-floor condo with a balcony overlooking a ravine. In previous apartments, I'd hang my hair to dry on a web of clotheslines rigged to the bathroom ceiling. Now I can sit on my balcony, lean back against the railing and look up toward the rooftop patio, one floor above.

That's how I met my upstairs neighbour. One afternoon, he came out to water his petunias and saw me sitting in the line of his spray nozzle. He stood at the edge and asked why I had my back to the view. I invited him down for dinner so he could see for himself. I think we were both taken by surprise. When I was his age, I wouldn't have had the nerve.

I learned that he's a chartered accountant who works from home. He bought his penthouse with the money he saved as a student while his peers were out partying. His parents are dead and he only listens to classical music.

Maybe my luck has finally caught up with me.

After years of prevention, starting a new relationship may seem reckless. Change can happen overnight, or you can slow it down.

Astrologers call your twenty-seventh year a Saturn return, and a lot of people don't make it. Jimi Hendrix, Janis Joplin, and Amy Winehouse all died at twenty-seven. And not just because of jazz.

I told my soon-to-be boyfriend what my real age is, and he thinks I'm joking. Even though there's no way my hair could be this long if I was close to being twenty-seven, like him. (He thinks it's extensions.)

The other day, he found his first grey strand. I asked him what he was going to do about it, and he said it didn't bother him. He explained that his father was bald by his age, so he has nothing to complain about.

I may be old enough to be his mother, but I can't shield him from the truth forever. It's time I let my hair down.

Model Shown Is Actual Size

1.

Last September, Imogen began work on a full-scale, three-dimensional replica of her rented bachelor apartment. The apartment was on the second floor of a seventies-style brown brick building north of campus. The replica was made entirely of corrugated cardboard, from boxes Imogen lugged home from the nearby Giant Tiger and liquor store. She cut out and glued on cardboard flaps and bent and stapled cardboard trusses. She painted every surface in painstaking, photographic detail with sable-hair brushes and acrylic paint: the gilded frame on a Cézanne poster, the floral print on wrinkled bedsheets, the warped reflections on the stainless-steel kettle.

Her landlord threatened to evict her if she got paint on any of the actual furnishings, though most of them looked like they had been there since the building was constructed.

Her tutor asked if she was making a postmodern comment on Dadaism.

"Umm," said Imogen, "I'm not sure if my work is really influenced by anything—at least, not intentionally, anyway."

Her tutor frowned and replied that that was impossible unless Imogen had been living in a bubble, that art by necessity must speak to the past as much as the future.

Imogen told him she would think about it, and went to weep over a beer in the student bar with her friend Andy.

"Why does there have to be a reason for everything?" Imogen wailed into her pint glass. "Why can't art just be beautiful?"

"You're doing your *whole* apartment?" said Andy. "Even the walls?"

Imogen planned to complete the architectural elements on site, in the student gallery. She painted the cardboard walls and the view through cardboard windows. She decided on a night view with the city's skyline silhouetted beneath the prairie sky, blue-black and littered with Van Gogh stars—white, orange, and yellow-gold.

She assured her tutors that her apartment in its entirety would still take up only one corner of the gallery. If her landlord did evict her, she decided, she would take refuge in her cardboard kingdom.

2.

Imogen held near and dear an image of her six-year-old self gleefully clutching fistfuls of coloured crayons, coaxed and nagged into literacy when she would much rather draw. Her parents imposed educational spelling bees that culminated in the challenge of her own name—she always got as far as the *g* and stopped. What was that many-lettered caterpillar crawling across the page? *I-m-o-g—I, mog.* She still signed her paintings "mog," as if those three letters could whisk back purple mountains, blue sunsets, and pink ponies long gone. Now, even the known world was disappearing. Her apartment, filled with cardboard reproductions of seventies furniture, was shrinking by the day. If she didn't stop soon, there'd be no room left to breathe.

3.

The day Imogen absentmindedly set her cardboard kettle alight when she put it on her electric stove, turned on the element and left the kitchen, was the day she realized she had gone too far. She was on the other side of the apartment, plumping cardboard cushions to make them look more inviting, when she smelled the smoke. She would have raced over were it not for the fact that her cardboard ceiling chose that moment to collapse. Imogen army-crawled her way through, and quelled the flames with an aluminum saucepan.

Afterwards, she searched through the debris for her sketchbook. She ripped out a fresh page and penned a letter in her best (though still wayward) cursive, informing Whom It May Concern that Imogen Sparks was ignoring her tutors' warnings and fulfilling her mid-term jury's predictions by dropping out of the undergraduate program in fine arts, just three weeks before fourth year finals.

Imogen slipped the folded letter into an envelope the hydro company had kindly provided along with her overdue bill, pulled on her windbreaker, and cycled to the dean's office. She handed the envelope to the dean's secretary, fled down Portage Avenue, and turned down Osborne Street, not stopping until she reached Roxxy's Nails and Spa.

Roxxy was on the phone behind the reception desk and glared at Imogen as if she might be a door-to-door salesperson.

"You want the mani–pedi?" snapped Roxxy. Her lips were syrup-coated cherries beneath a peroxide moustache.

"Actually," said Imogen, "I was wondering if I could just have my toenails done."

"Cheaper to do both," scowled Roxxy. "It's fifteen for the pedi."

Imogen had biked past Roxxy's many times before. The sign in the window said "Mani-Pedi $25 Special" but Imogen never had a spare twenty-five dollars. Besides, she had a good eye and steady hand and was perfectly capable of painting her own nails. She thought of the twenty-dollar bill she had withdrawn from the ATM that morning. Her balance was now minus $283.79 and her credit card bill was even worse.

"No, really. I'm an artist and I work with my hands," lied Imogen. She held up her short, bitten fingernails. Her fingers were peeling with dried Krazy Glue and scabbed from minor X-Acto knife accidents. "Anyway, I just want a splash of colour—a token symbol for the end of an era."

"Break-up?" said Roxxy.

"Uhh, kind of," said Imogen. "We're just taking a break till I figure a few things out."

4.

No one phoned or texted Imogen all week to ask why she wasn't at school, a hive of caffeine- and music-fuelled industry as the year-end juries approached. Imogen stayed home eating Bran Flakes and Mr. Noodles, surrounded by fragments of non-functional furniture, which made moving around the apartment almost impossible.

She retreated to her closet to compile an outfit befitting her new life and impeccable pedicure. Unfortunately, all her clothes were faded shades of black with paint-splatters, rips, and missing buttons. Her wardrobe screamed *I am an art student*. She decided it was best not to get dressed at all.

On the weekend, Andy called. They had slept together, briefly, in first year. This was during Andy's experimental phase, when he thought he might not be gay after all but really bisexual. Andy painted male nudes almost exclusively but narrowly avoided being accused of anachronism by slashing some of his canvases, ripping staples out of others, and stamping them with the soles of his size thirteen Doc Martens (which he wore with two pairs of insoles).

"I haven't heard from you all week," said Andy. "What are you doing?"

Imogen considered telling Andy that she was lying naked on her green velvet couch eating Smartfood, but didn't want to risk further rejection.

"Just hanging out," she said. "Admiring my pedicure."

"Since when do you go for pedis?" said Andy. "I've been trying to get us to go on a spa date for, like, ever."

Andy had been the one who said, "I'm sorry Mogs, but this just isn't working out."

"Don't you even want to try?" Imogen had sobbed. "You might change your mind again."

Whenever Imogen saw Andy, she looked for traces of the skinny boy with the Woody Allen eyebrows whom she'd fallen in love with at the frosh-week beer pong game. It was hard to spot him now in the tattooed gym rat who had become her best friend and still invited her for sleepovers. Imogen tried not to look too hard for traces of the past and its unfulfilled promises. She closed her eyes and embraced the edgy yet soft-spoken present with its abs of steel.

"It's like, two weeks before our finals and you're home painting your toenails," said Andy.

"*I* didn't paint them," said Imogen. "Art and I are on a break. I'm not picking up a paintbrush again until I've figured out what to do with my life."

"But we're artists," said Andy. "It's in our blood. It's not something we can un-choose."

Imogen stood in front of her closet mirror and asked her naked self, *Did I choose art? Why did I choose art?* She wiggled her toes and they winked cheerfully back at her in bright neon pink.

5.

Andy came over the next evening on his way home from the gym. Imogen threw on her vintage kimono and ran downstairs to open the door because the buzzer did not work. Imogen suspected it had never worked and was in fact a display model the landlord had glued to the wall.

"This is ridiculous," said Andy. "I am not letting you quit."

"It's too late," said Imogen.

"You're so close to finishing," said Andy. "Why give up now?"

"I'm sick of having to justify myself to everyone," said Imogen. "Everyone hates my work. I hate my work."

"We all go through that," said Andy. "I look at myself in the mirror some days and think, *Who's that fat bitch?*" He pulled up his Abercrombie & Fitch hoodie to reveal his tanned stomach, so taut you could stretch canvas on it.

Imogen tightened the belt on her kimono and wished she had at least put on some underwear. She said, "Why does everything have to be about you? What I'm saying is, if you're not doing some kind of interdisciplinary performance art involving nudity and/or bodily fluids, you're nobody in the art world these days."

"Oh honey, please," said Andy. "What art world? If you mean this quaint town, well, who cares? Move to Montreal with me."

"I thought you hated Montreal."

Andy was from Laval, which he insisted was like every Winnipeg suburb, with even worse winters—it wasn't the actual temperature but the dampness of the cold that ate into your bones. Here, you could go club hopping in ripped jeans, a leather bomber, and a mesh muscle shirt, and you'd just feel numb, maybe get a little frostbite at the worst. Except there was nowhere to go.

"We'll get an apartment in the Village," said Andy. "Party central, here we come."

"But my French is terrible."

"You can be the mysterious artiste."

"Just look at my work," said Imogen, gesturing around the room, almost knocking over her wine glass with her kimono sleeve. "Do you really think anyone is going to like it? Do you even like it?"

They sat in silence and surveyed the remnants of Imogen's artistic career.

"Oh hey," said Andy. "Nice toenails."

"Do you think they're too pink?" She extended both legs and pointed her toes.

Already, there was a tiny chip on her right pinkie toenail. Imogen decided she would give herself as long as her pedicure lasted to figure out a plan. If she didn't come up with a better solution, she would seriously consider taking Andy up on his offer.

6.

Imogen spent the summer working in a small coffee shop on Arthur Street. It was so far off the beaten track that the manager in desperation lugged a sandwich board to Main Street, a block away, in the hope of luring customers to the quiet enclave of abandoned warehouses and ancient trees where the café was located. Even at the busiest times, there never seemed to be more than one or two customers.

Imogen whiled away the hours sipping chai lattes and wondering when she was going to find her path in life. She started seeing a poet who came in at lunchtime every day and ordered the egg salad sandwich on rye. He told her she was beautiful and asked if she'd ever considered being a model.

"No," said Imogen.

"If I were an artist, I would paint you," said the poet.

"I used to be an artist," said Imogen.

"But I'm only a poet," the poet continued sadly. "My words could never capture the essence of your beauty, especially your eyes."

He made a list of metaphors for her particular shade of green in his notebook, and showed them to Imogen: sea glass, emerald, clover.

"How about just saying green," said Imogen. "Or pink—it's such a happy colour."

"But so unsophisticated," said the poet.

They went on meandering bike rides along the Red River like lovers in a French art movie. Imogen wore a red vintage sundress with white polka dots which she'd found at Ragpickers Antifashion Emporium.

Once, the poet braked abruptly with a squeal of skidding tires, pitched his bike on the grassy bank, and hastily pulled out his notebook and pen.

"What's wrong?" asked Imogen.

"Shh," said the poet who was sitting on the grass, brow furrowed, notebook open to his most recent unfinished poem, tentatively titled "Portrait of I." "Don't say anything or you'll scare it off."

He had crossed out and replaced words so many times that the page looked like an abstract sketch by Franz Kline.

"It?" said Imogen. Lately, she'd begun to wonder if his increasing resemblance to Vincent Van Gogh—he'd started growing a reddish beard and moustache to get a head start on Movember—was legitimate grounds for concern about his sanity.

"I had the perfect line and now it's gone," he muttered to himself.

Imogen lay on the grass, chewing a stalk of clover. She watched the poet's black-rimmed glasses descend by increments down the bridge of his nose and was glad she wasn't an artist anymore.

Afterwards, they went back to Imogen's apartment, drank wine and listened to Górecki's Third Symphony.

"Don't you get hot in here?" complained the poet. "You should recycle some of that cardboard; it's blocking the airflow."

He lived in a shared house where there was always cat hair on the couch and a jazz jam in the basement. Imogen had visited once and told him she was allergic to cats and jazz.

"Then take off your shirt," suggested Imogen. "That's what I do."

"It's all right for *you*," said the poet, with longing. He was pale and narrow-chested with hairy shoulders and a beginning stoop.

Whenever they were in bed together, he insisted on turning all the lights off. Imogen listened to the poet's breathing grow short and urgent, like a pig snuffling around in its feeding trough. She kept her sundress on. What was the good of not looking when you knew what was there?

7.

Imogen told the poet she wanted to be alone, free to wander naked around her apartment without the presence of an objectifying eye.

In the evenings, she lay silently in the dark with the windows wide open and relished her secret nakedness. All around her, stray cardboard cut-outs and tottering follies swayed with the evening breeze. She listened to the rustling of beaded curtains and spider plants, and the persistent creaks and whispers from fragments of her former art project, which she hadn't had the heart to crush and consign to the recycling bin. She studied their lumpy silhouettes among her landlord's mismatched furniture, and tried to guess which was which. Success was not being able to tell them apart. Not that it mattered, now that her creations would never be displayed. They would be spared the scrutiny of unforgiving eyes: the shifty, leering gaze of art critics; the mocking, sidewise glance of peers; the bored disdain of her tutors.

Imogen wasn't the only one who felt relieved. The cardboard toaster oven muttered, begrudgingly, that at least its painted buttons wouldn't be pressed, its painted bagel never criticized for being underdone. The cardboard closet admitted it was probably for the best—it would be spared the embarrassment of being opened to reveal that it hid no cardboard skeletons. Only the painted picture frames grumbled at being denied their moment of glory on opening night, without which their existence felt somewhat meaningless.

Their murmurs rose each time a breeze swept through. Imogen rolled onto her stomach and put her fingers in her ears. She lay still until the silence in her head expanded to fill the entire room, engulfing everything in its path, flowing outwards through the open windows into a bottomless sky. She felt as though she had finally escaped the outside world and was lying in the cradle of a cosmic womb, waiting to be reborn.

8.

Andy was having his first solo show at Zsa Zsa Gallery in Chinatown, opposite the all-night restaurant where the cops line up for dim sum on a break in their night shift. Andy had arranged for the subject of his paintings to lounge naked in the gallery on opening night, recreating the compositions in a live tableau.

Imogen wore her kimono over a black lace minidress and tried to avoid former classmates. When cornered, she told them she was resting on doctor's orders after contracting tendonitis from too much painting.

After the guests left, Imogen and the artist's model helped clear the empty beer bottles and cigarette butts off the side-walk in front of the gallery. Andy invited them to share the last of the wine on the roof of the building, accessed via the second-floor washroom through a door marked with graffiti that read: What happens in Vegas stays in Vegas.

They sat on the black-tarred rooftop, dangled their legs over the eavestrough, and shared an enormous Cuban cigar that the model produced from the pocket of his distressed jeans.

"Cheers," said Andy, raising his red plastic beer cup. "To Marco, the star of the show." He wrapped an arm around the model's waist.

"Nice job," said Imogen. She wasn't sure whom she should be complimenting. "So, Marco—what do you do when you're not modelling?"

Marco half turned his Grecian profile and exhaled an aromatic grey cloud.

"I like to sing," he said. "Play some guitar, like Mexican rock and roll, you know?"

"Not really," said Imogen.

"He's got a beautiful voice," interrupted Andy, pulling
Marco closer. "We're going to start a band and I'm going to
be his go-go dancer."

"Okay, but seriously," said Imogen. "How do you make a
living?"

"You're just jealous," said Andy. "Wouldn't we all like to get
paid to lie around naked, looking beautiful? Marco has an
artistic soul. He's just taking some time to figure a few things
out, living in the moment. He's coming with me to Montreal."

Montreal. Hadn't it been their plan—Andy and Imogen,
best friends for life?

"Well thanks for telling me," said Imogen. She hated how
her voice sounded, like the poet's reproachful whining: *I
thought you liked being my muse.*

"Well I'm telling you now," said Andy. "You can come and
crash on our couch anytime."

Marco's face was hidden, nestled against Andy's shoulder.
Occasionally, puffs of smoke rose from below Andy's right
earlobe as if his biker jacket was on fire.

"Thanks," said Imogen, "but I don't know when I'll have
the time. It's going to get really busy with my show coming
up and everything."

"What show?" said Andy.

Even Marco looked up, cigar arrested between slim fingers,
pale blue eyes framed by blue-black ringlets. Imogen had
to admit they were a good-looking couple, straight out of
a Guess ad.

"My work's just been sitting at home for months and I
need to get it off my back. Finish that chapter. Find closure,
I suppose."

"That's awesome, Mogs," said Andy. His smile was wide, genuine—gone was the studied cool he'd spent the better part of his university years cultivating. "When's opening night?"

"Oh, you'll be in Montreal by then," said Imogen vaguely. The evening air was nipping at the hem of her lace dress and she rubbed her arms through the thin silk sleeves of her kimono.

"We haven't booked our bus tickets yet," Andy persisted. "We'd love to be there. Let me know if there's anything we can do."

Imogen felt the warmth of the wine spreading through her, despite the coolness of the September evening. Soon it would be fall again—the first autumn in memory that she wouldn't be in school.

"I'll let you know if I need any help," she said. "It's going to be really small. Like, *really* small."

The sight of her bare legs dangling over the edge of the roof above the car park, deserted but for a lone police car, was making her dizzy. She took another gulp from the red plastic cup.

"Actually, I was thinking of having it in my apartment."

9.

Imogen resumed work on her abandoned final year project, hesitantly at first (was it really such a good idea to follow through on a drunken whim blurted out in pride and jealousy?). The first time she picked up her paintbrushes, their slim wooden handles felt as awkward as chopsticks between her fingers. But as the paint flowed and the colours on her palette merged with each other and birthed new colours, the distinctions between model and sculpture, artist and creation, began to dissolve. Imogen put aside her paintbrushes and used her fingers to smear, stroke, and mould colour and light in kaleidoscopic patterns, directly onto cardboard. She felt like a mermaid disguised as a girl, whose legs had turned back into fins and a tail as soon as they touched water.

As her body of work grew, her apartment shrank proportionally. Even the cardboard walls seemed to take up more space than Imogen had imagined a two-dimensional plane would occupy. She made flyers with the date, time, address, and title: *Not-So-Obscure Objects of Desire*. She pinned the flyers to notice boards in galleries, second-hand bookstores, even the Giant Tiger.

On opening night, Andy and Marco helped Imogen put the final touches to the apartment. Marco had brought flowers and Imogen explained, apologetically, that she'd have to leave them in the dingy downstairs vestibule—every object on display needed its cardboard counterpart. Many of the pieces were unfinished but Andy said it didn't matter, it was a comment on the creative process. Andy and Marco went to the liquor store, promising to return before the guests arrived.

Though it was early October, the city was in the grip of an unexpected heatwave. The apartment was warm as a toaster oven and Imogen was sweating in her black sleeveless tunic, opaque pantyhose, and ballet flats. ("We're Andy Warhol and Edie Sedgwick!" Andy had exclaimed, enfolding her in a bony hug, and it was almost as though nothing had changed.)

Imogen collapsed onto her couch and kicked off her shoes. This is the worst idea ever, she thought. No one's going to come. Everyone's going to hate this show.

She jumped up, ran to the front door, and drew the bolt across. She turned out all the lights and sat down again in the dark. If she didn't make a noise, perhaps people would think the show was cancelled and there was no one home.

With the lights out, it felt slightly cooler but Imogen tore off her tunic and hurled it in a crumpled ball onto the replica couch. The cardboard swayed and groaned under the force of the impact. Next, she peeled off her pantyhose and underwear and flung those on top of the tunic. Then she threw herself down on her green velvet couch and curled into a ball. She wished she was having a quiet night at home, eating Mr. Noodles and watching old episodes of *Will and Grace* on YouTube. She wished Andy wasn't moving to Montreal. She wished she had loved the poet, even a little, because in truth he had bored and saddened her—for his love of limericks, for an adulation of Irving Layton that amounted to plagiarism, for arguing that Andy Warhol was the American equivalent of Pablo Picasso, for preferring Wagner to Brahms—for not being a true artist.

Imogen would have cried if she could. When she tired of squeezing her eyes shut as tightly as possible, wrapping her arms around her knees, rocking from side to side, and whimpering softly, she sat on the edge of her couch with her head in her hands, and opened her eyes. From behind the painted windows, through a gap between the cardboard wall and window frame, seeped a streetlamp's electric moonlight—a pale blue trickle flowing to Imogen's feet. For the past month, she had barely had any time to look in a mirror. Her body had followed her around and sometimes helped, mostly got in the way, during the merciless countdown to opening night. Cautiously, she dipped her feet in the puddle of light and wiggled her toes. Only one of them winked back:

on the outermost tip of her left big toe was a crescent-shaped scrap of pink pigment. It seemed impossible, but it was there.

The buzzer rang. An urgent, bleating sound Imogen didn't recognize. Had the landlord finally installed a new, working model? It must be the neighbour's.

Imogen kept looking at her toes. How much longer would the nail polish last? Another day? week? month? Each time she had tried to guess, she had been wrong. The nail polish had exceeded all her expectations. Perhaps it would last forever. *It's not too late*, thought Imogen.

The buzzer rang again, accompanied by thumping on the downstairs door. Voices floated up from the street. The bleating was clearly happening inside her apartment, and it was definitely coming from that small, wall-mounted plastic speaker—or was it the cardboard one right beside it?

Imogen rose and reached for her trusty kimono. Knotting the sash securely at her waist, she unlocked her front door and opened it. The cooler air from the corridor stirred the kimono's silky folds, and Imogen's skin tingled expectantly.

Before she turned on the lights, she glanced behind her once more. There was her apartment and its shadowy contents arranged two-by-two, everything appearing twice as if with a long-lost twin. Though overstuffed and impractical, the place felt cozy and complete as it never had before. Then Imogen caught her breath, for in the darkened doorway to the bathroom, where the light from the corridor did not reach, she glimpsed a dim silhouette. When she raised her hand to the light switch, the figure did not move. Imogen looked down at her bare feet, sticky against the linoleum tiles. She knew that the moment she flicked the light switch on, that other Imogen would be gone.

Quartet for the New Generation

GIRLHOOD

My son likes dressing as a girl; he can't help it, and neither can I.

I've tried. Periwinkle-blue corduroy dungarees; pistachio-striped seersucker pyjamas; a Little Lord Fauntleroy jacket with tiny gold buttons, paired with buckle-up shoes (Ollie loved his page-boy haircut, but insisted on wearing it in a half ponytail). Even if we could afford to shop handmade, local, and organic, Ollie's not fooled by minimalist, unisex fashions. Each year it gets harder to reconcile our opposing desires. (Mine: to protect him from ridicule or worse.)

I'm in Walmart browsing the monster masks and Ollie's two racks away, checking out the fairy wings and tiaras.

This guy's cute, I say, picking out a green-faced ghoul that looks like a cross between Frankenstein and E.T.—the latest Disney character, perhaps, or another obscure superhero dredged up by Hollywood in hopes of repeating the inexplicable success of last year's *Iron Man*.

In the months leading up to Ollie's birth, my parents bought him a welcome gift: two sets of onesies, one pink, one blue. Upon learning the gender of their new grandchild, they promptly tried to return the pink one to The Bay. Luckily for Ollie, the thirty-day window had passed. The onesies were two sizes larger than newborn (thanks to immigrant thriftiness), and he was still wearing them when he learned his first words. Bye, bye, he'd chant, waving vigorously, whenever

I got out the blue one. At the time, I couldn't see the difference—both onesies had pompon ears and appliqué hearts.

Now he's six, and clothing companies seem to think that Grade One qualifies all little boys to be outfitted as miniature bankers or B-boys.

Thank goodness for Halloween.

The snot-green plastic crinkles when I pull at the mask's elastic and attempt to slide it over Ollie's chestnut tangles.

Ow, he complains, pushing me away.

He's tall for his age, and strong. Give him another half-decade or so and he'll outstrip me and his father. It's the hormones they pump into all those hot dogs he eats. They don't even resemble real meat, but I haven't been able to convince him. And forget about compromising with veggie dogs. I'd never let him eat junk, but I remember how hard I begged my parents for a taste of normal, non-Chinese food.

Ollie rips off the mask and shoves it into my hands.

Elphaba, he says disdainfully.

What's the matter? Don't you like him?

It's a *her*. Don't you know?

How could I have forgotten the avocado-skinned witch from *Wicked*, the musical my parents took him to last year?— an odd choice for a five-year-old, when the only theatre they ever took me to was the Beijing Opera. Perhaps Elphaba's fantastical visage reminded them of the brightly painted masks of Chinese mythological characters. Ollie's first visit to the theatre sparked an obsession that his grandparents indulged with the purchase of the original Broadway cast recording, posters, and songbook. My carefully curated collection of sleepy-time tunes—*Eine Kleine Nachtmusik, Peter and the Wolf*—was lost in the CD player's shuffle. Eventually, Ollie's attentions were claimed by a community production

of *Joseph and the Amazing Technicolour Dreamcoat*, and the
tie-dye caftan he begged me to buy from Kensington Market.
This year, the Christmas production is *Anne of Green Gables*.
Ollie was heartbroken to learn that they were only casting
grades four and up, but that hasn't stopped him from rehearsing in our living room—he's memorized all the songs.

I hurry after Ollie and find him entranced before a selec-
tion of wigs and hairpieces that wouldn't be out of place
on a Vegas stage. On the lowest shelf: a row of femme-fatale
helmets in rainbow colours. Ollie gently finger-combs the
purple one, then points at the shelf above, where a cascade
of wheat-field golden curls crowns a Styrofoam head.

Try it on, Rose! He sneaks a sideways glance.

I haven't had long hair since he was born. My post-preg-
nancy pixie cut, inspired by Faye Wong in *Chungking Express*,
shocked my parents almost as much as when, twelve months
later, they heard their grandson address his parents by our
first names.

That's not my colour, I say, and place the wig in his outstretched hands. You try it on.

Okay! he says, clearly relieved.

Who taught him to fish for approval when I give it so
readily? Frank and I spoil Ollie; our emphasis is on positive
reinforcement. I've been choking back the word *no* ever since
he first tried to climb out of his crib only to topple back in
head first, landing with a soft thump. These small failures
probably hurt me more than him, but I couldn't bring myself
to thwart his instinct for freedom.

What about you? says Ollie, ever thoughtful, not want-
ing me to be left out. I hope that unconditional love will
keep the doors of his heart wide open long after he realizes
there must be someone else out there who'd make a better

accomplice in his dress-up games. He tugs at my folded arms.
What colour do you like?

The wigs hang in limp rows like docked ponies' tails.

This one, I say, reaching for a set of rust-red braids. Do you
think I could be Anne?

Over here, says Ollie. He hauls me toward a mirror at
the end of the aisle, skipping and singing in an angelic,
head-turning soprano. The mirror's too narrow for us to
stand side by side before it and see both ourselves and each
other. Ollie darts forward, wig in hand, then hesitates, suddenly shy.

. Go on, I say. I step behind him and slip the blonde wig
over his ears. Then I place the red one on my head and flick
the pigtails over my shoulders. The asymmetric ends of my
layered bob stick out underneath. I look and feel ridiculous,
and the elasticated mesh cap chafes my ears.

Pretty, says Ollie. He twirls his imaginary gown.

Very pretty, I say, wishing I could summon half his innocence and enthusiasm, hoping he won't notice when I can't.

Already he's dancing back down the aisle, rummaging
through the gowns and tutus. I need a costume to match.

Let's go pay for the wigs, I say. I have to raise my voice to
reach him, and I don't care who hears it. You have plenty of
dresses at home.

I'll give Ollie anything he wants, but I know when
enough's enough.

BOYHOOD

Before Rosie, I didn't know dim sum from bibimbap. For our first date, I took her to Swiss Chalet.

My parents hate this stuff, she said in between slurps of gravy. They are so Chinese.

I don't think I've ever had real Chinese food, I told her. Like those secret dishes they leave off the English menu?

Rosie raised her elegantly arched brows. They looked natural to me, unlike the plucked, shaved and redrawn exclamation marks on some of our fellow classmates. Most of them had a crush on the well-known male poet teaching First-Year Seminar: Pulp Fictions that year. I was seriously thinking of dropping his elective because the excessive grooming he inspired meant that the already stuffy air in the auditorium was thick with perfumes that set off my allergies. Refreshingly, Rosie didn't seem to buy into commercial notions of beauty. Sitting across the table from her now, all I could smell was the roast chicken.

What did you grow up on, Frank—KFC?

In time, I'd figure out that straight-faced sarcasm usually meant that Rosie was in a flirtatious mood, though it remained near-impossible to tell when she was actually being serious. When I didn't reply, she put her hand over her mouth and giggled: Oh my God, I'm so sorry.

All I could think was: I can't believe I'm on a date with Myca from *The Crow*. Before Rosie, I'd never realized the difference between Mandarin and Cantonese Chinese.

She later claimed that if she didn't trim her brows, she'd resemble one of those ancient Chinese sages whose unchecked facial hair was a sign of longevity. She also had an impressive collection of lipsticks in what looked like the same muted pink, but refused manicures and mascara. Her contradictions were fascinating and familiar, superlatively human.

The first time we kissed, I cupped her face gingerly with frozen fingers, amazed that she would let me get this close to her. We'd just been to see *Before Sunrise* and Rosie had joked that we should spend the rest of the night wandering the downtown streets like we were in Vienna, even though it was early April and barely above zero. I interrupted our flâneuring to pull her down beside me on a bench on Philosopher's Walk.

Your skin is so soft, I whispered in awe.

Rosie freed herself from my hesitant pawing. I won't break, she said. I'm not some china doll.

That's not what I meant. I felt myself blush. Luckily, we were a safe distance from the frosted light of the nearest wrought iron lamp.

You're not one of those guys who only dates Asians, are you?

No, I am not a rice king.

You know that term? She sounded impressed.

Relieved, I leaned closer. I do have Asian friends, you know, I mumbled to her neck. We live in, like, the most multicultural city in the world.

Toronto's pretty great, I guess.

I think you're pretty great, too.

She sighed. I hoped it was with anticipation; she was probably rolling her eyes.

After one year of dating, Rosie introduced me to her parents over lunch in a Markham restaurant decked with hanging lanterns and silk orchids. I still salivate, recalling my first taste of Peking Duck. By then, Rosie had turned vegan and refused to touch even the bed of shredded lettuce the duck was presented on. Her mom smiled excessively, piled our plates with food, and ignored the fact that Rosie shovelled most of hers onto my plate. Rosie's dad chatted about current affairs and asked what I thought of Canada's immigration policy.

It's great, I said. Since most Canadians actually come from somewhere else, those of us who were born here feel cooler by default.

Rosie speared a slippery black mushroom with one chopstick and said, Dad doesn't think he's Canadian.

Rosie's dad cleared his throat and said, Hong Kong was part of the British Commonwealth until 1997.

Canada still is, Rosie muttered.

My mom's from Scotland and my dad's from Ireland, I said, unsure whether this excused me from colonial crimes, or further implicated me.

More tea for you, Frank? said her mom.

On the subway back to town, Rosie said: When I have kids I'm going to let them do whatever they want.

A vision of Rosie cradling a dark-haired, blue-eyed baby flashed into view then disappeared, like the blur of suburban tenements and cul-de-sacs outside the window. I was glad when we plunged back into underground darkness.

Your parents seem pretty liberal, I said. I mean, they don't seem to mind you shacking up with some white guy.

They have no choice, Rosie said in the same mild yet implacable voice her mom had used when asking about my plans after graduation.

I decided that this wasn't the best time to ask for Rosie's views on arranged marriage and was that a Hong Kong tradition. She'd pulled out a spiral-bound notebook from her coat pocket and was flipping through its pages, many of which were coming loose.

Feeling inspired? I didn't expect an answer. She was clearly about to disappear into one of her bouts of spontaneous writing—chasing a poem, she called it.

I picked up a newspaper from a nearby seat and scanned the movie listings. Could I convince her to watch the new *Star Trek* with me? After all, I'd agreed to *The English Patient* even though I'd had to read the book (for Literary Anthropology: Colonial Fictions), and the dialogue's as stiff as Hemingway's.

I never want to look at another spring roll again, Rosie said suddenly. My brain's deep fried.

The golden, vegetable-stuffed rolls had been the only vegan appetizer on the menu, served dripping with hot oil, which cancelled out any potential health benefits.

But it was so worth it, I said. The memory of steamed lobster wafted through my mind on a garlic-infused cloud.

You don't understand, said Rosie. It's rude not to eat. They don't care whether or not you like it.

Graduate school came and went. Applying for doctoral scholarships seemed like the most plausible way to ensure the continuation of our precarious yet reassuringly familiar student lifestyle. Meanwhile, Rosie was working eleven-hour shifts at Starbucks. I told myself we'd made the right choice. That Rosie, being the talented one, was born to publish poetry collections, not theses. Whereas my own writing skills only served to prove that I was eminently unemployable.

One evening, I came home from an afternoon spent exploring the rare book library to find Rosie lying on our apartment floor, surrounded by copies of the handmade chapbook she'd self-published six years ago, in first year. The chapbooks lay open to different pages, like SOS missives from the fallout of some literary bomb.

I've hit rock bottom, she said. Today the manager asked me to write a limerick that used the words *mocha* and *cocoa*. In coloured chalk.

Let's go out for dinner, I said. My treat.

My parents were right, she said. I should have become an engineer. Or married one.

I tried not to take it personally. Lately, Rosie had been irritable and moody. She hadn't written a poem in months, and I suspected that this was the heart of the problem. I couldn't remember the last time I'd opened the bathroom cabinet, or my Edwardian faux wood and ivory cigarette case (scored at the St. Lawrence Antique Market), to discover one of her Post-it note haikus. Now the missives tacked to the fridge door and kitchen table carried grocery lists or terse one-liners: *Back at ten*, or *Call your mom*.

How about sushi? I said. We could go to Mariko's, or New Generation.

Rosie was still vegetarian but had started eating fish again.

You choose, she said. Just not the place with the Ikea rice paper screens, please.

We sat by the window and ordered bento boxes and sake. I tried to entertain her by talking about my potential thesis topics, most of which were already starting to bore me. I was in the middle of a tangential rant about how niche specialization in subaltern or gender studies seemed to be key to getting a research topic approved—a bit of a problem when the only thing marginalized about the Medieval manuscripts that fascinated me were the unexpected asides left behind by anonymous scribes ("the parchment is hairy" or "St. Patrick of Armagh, deliver me from writing")—when Rosie looked up from the plate of discarded edamame skins she'd been picking at for most of the evening. She hadn't said much so far, and I welcomed the chance to grab a bite of blood-red, white-striped tuna.

I'm happy for you, Frank, she said. You're following your heart.

Her smile looked a little wan, but it could have been the lighting.

No, no, I'm just lucky, I said. If it wasn't for you ...

I stopped. I was getting choked up and my mouth was full of sashimi.

Do you think, said Rosie, after you finish your thesis, maybe you'd want to, um, get married?

Sure, I said, then immediately hoped I didn't look as surprised as I felt. In six years' worth of dinner conversations, marriage had never come up before, though I sometimes worried about what her parents thought.

Oh my God, said Rosie, and burst into tears. I thought you'd never ask me.

She blew her nose loudly into her napkin, while I filched a fresh one from a nearby table.

Had her question been an actual proposal? Was I ready? Would I ever be?

Maybe it didn't matter. For years, I'd been bracing myself to turn the next corner and run smack into the rest of our lives. Now the future was settled and the weight of burgeoning responsibility thrown off, left to the past.

We'd slipped, for once, into the present: a Bloor Street night in November, lit by the caustic light of street lamps hung with icicles. I looked out at the snow-swept scene and pictured the walk home—Rosie's hand warm in mine, nestled in my pocket. The draught from the window sliced through my stiff, dark jeans and flannel long johns, raising the hairs on my legs. I inhaled sharply.

Cold? said Rosie.

I shook my head. This is going to sound crazy, I said, but I feel like taking off my clothes and running naked through the snow.

Rosie grinned and started waving madly for the waiter, who was nowhere to be seen. At that moment, I fully believed that the force of her will might be enough to summon our cheque.

I'll race you, she said.

FRIENDSHIP

Is it wrong of me to spend more time texting Nathan than playing Super Smash Bros. on the flat-screen in the rec room down the hall with the other guys? I've tried, but I can't see the point. It's just a bunch of cartoon characters with cute names punching, kicking, slashing, and shooting each other to a pulp like they're auditioning for the next Tarantino movie.

Hey Nathan, what's up?

Not much

Wanna drop out of school and go on a road trip?

With who?

R u serious?

If we were in the same room, having a real conversation, I'd probably punch him in the arm, and he'd act mortally wounded till I apologized. But Nathan's back home in Toronto, and the person I talk to the most now IRL is my roommate Tyler.

For the record, I don't usually do online-only friendships. I don't feel comfortable expressing myself through text, where there's so much room for misinterpretation. You have to be in the same room to read a person's body language, to know how they're feeling. But since I moved to Winnipeg, I've had a lot of practice—I don't have much choice.

Now, when I'm chatting with Nathan, it almost feels like he's here. We've been friends since Grade Two, when we were the only mixed kids in our class. His mom's Korean and mine's Chinese, not that anyone can tell the difference. We've always liked the same kinds of food, comics, and Japanese stuffed toys.

Which is why I can tell what mood he's in even when we're on WhatsApp.

Right now, Nathan's distracted. He's probably playing Minecraft on his iPad. At least with Minecraft, you can build your own tropical island and teleport there whenever you want.

Should I go play Super Smash in the rec room?

With who?

Everyone

Even Tyler?

Ya

Tyler's hot

Tyler's bed is at the other end of our narrow dorm. He gets the window because he's been here for four years now, and I only joined last September. Nathan keeps asking me if Tyler's gay, but I haven't decided yet. I don't know him that well, though he's the closest to being an actual friend.

The other guys here, in Level Seven of the Professional Division, don't even count. We clump together in the cafeteria out of necessity: because we are only five, and there are sixteen girls.

I'm probably the oldest person who's ever joined the Ballet Academic Program, when other students my age are getting ready to graduate. *Long legs and neck, classical aesthetic, rhythm and drive*, the jury wrote on my audition report. You have to be willing to adapt, they said, when I went in with my parents for the final interview. It could be quite a shock.

My dad said: Are you sure this is what you want, Oliver?

My mom said: As long as you're happy.

Then they took me out for a celebratory dinner at East Side Mario's. I wanted to tell them I wasn't sure what I wanted and had no idea how I felt, or if happiness is actually possible. But I didn't, because then they would have asked why I was doing this, and my only answer would have been: Because I know I can. That's what I told the jury, and they seemed impressed. I'm not sure why I said that. All I knew was, it would probably be the hardest thing I'd ever tried.

After dinner, my parents dropped me off at Nathan's place.

What's that? said Nathan as soon as I walked in. He was looking at the brown paper envelope in my hands.

I got in! I said, waving it gingerly—I was trying not to crease the letter inside, in case my mom wanted to add it to the collection.

Woo-hoo, said Nathan, let's celebrate!

I was too stuffed to move, but he put on Scissor Sisters, a retro band he got into after seeing their lead singer's solo show at the Mod Club last November (he made me tell his parents we were having a study night), and started doing the cancan to "I Don't Feel Like Dancin'." Then he collapsed on his purple beanbag and held out his hand.

Okay, you can show me now.

Show you what?

Ollie, said Nathan, with mock disapproval. You're supposed to be, like, super excited.

Oh, you mean the audition report, I said, and handed him the envelope.

Nathan read the whole thing without saying a word. He didn't even smile or say *Mmm!* like my mom did when she got to the good parts. Then he passed it back without looking at me, and shrugged.

Well duh, he said. I could have told you that.

I used to think that serious conversations bored Nathan, till I read somewhere that yawning can be a sign of stress in dogs—maybe it applied to humans too.

So what do you think? Should I do it?

Why not?

Because Winnipeg's a billion miles away from everyone. Because you're my best friend, and we wouldn't get to hang out. Because sometimes I think we're two sides of the same person.

I don't know, I said. It's like, a professional school. They take ballet pretty seriously.

What do your parents think?

Frank's cool with it, or seems to be—he doesn't have a clue about ballet. I know Rose doesn't want me to go, but she'd never say anything.

Nathan rolled off his purple beanbag and started searching for the remote.

If it doesn't work out, you can always come back.

Would you want me to?

You haven't even gone yet, he said, and changed the track to Tori Amos.

Last summer, Nathan dragged me to a model agency's casting call in a repurposed warehouse down by Lakeshore. The warehouse was a twenty-minute walk from the nearest bus stop, and by the time we arrived, we were sweating. Of the handful of guys lined up outside the crumbling building, alongside a flock of anorexic-looking girls, we must have been the least athletic or "cut."

It's not fair, said Nathan when he came back outside, after the short-lived suspense of making it as far as the second round. Girls get to look like wire coat hangers, and we're supposed to work out.

I was relieved that we hadn't been called back for further test shots. The USA IBC finals were streaming that afternoon, and I couldn't wait to get home and watch the cream of the ballet world pouring their bodies in and out of shapes I can almost approximate, now that I practise five hours a day.

On the way back from the warehouse, I thought about hitchhiking, then I wondered what kind of person would pick us up. Nathan had taken off his sweat-soaked shirt and was practising his catwalk strut.

We just don't have a mainstream look, I said in what I hoped was a conciliatory tone, repeating what the talent scout had said as she ushered me out. But don't worry—five years from now, when China takes over the world, we'll be the face of the new generation.

In five years we'll be *ancient,* said Nathan with disgust. Then he added, Well, at least we have Asian genes—we'll still *look* like we're seventeen.

Nathan once made us watch Visconti's *Death in Venice.* I fell asleep in the middle and promised him I'd make up for it by reading the book, but though I got at least three quarters of the way through before giving up, I never reached the part where the narrator actually meets Tadzio, the boy he's obsessed with—which made no sense to me. How can you get so hung up on someone you've never met in person? It was worth it, though, for the impressed look on my dad's face when he saw me reading Thomas Mann.

Not that he ever said anything about it. It's like my parents got used to me being a straight-A student who also happens to be athletic and musical, so they don't expect anything less. My granddad says it's the Chinese work ethic, but that only accounts for fifty percent. The truth is, everything came easy before ballet. I'd been taking figure skating lessons since Grade Five, so it was a pretty smooth transition to dance.

Most kids start with classical, which gives them a strong foundation. I started with tap and jazz, and moved on to ballet when a teacher told me I'd never be a real artist if I didn't have to suffer for it. Even at that age, I understood that no one really values what they don't have to fight for—my granddad was right about that.

Plié, relevé, tombé, arabesque—keep the legs turned out, Olivier! Don't twist them about! Ms. Dianova screams all day until I stop hearing her words. You should be so tired by the end of my class, you have to crawl back to your bed.

My body feels like an old man's, I tell Nathan. *I hate ballet* *You could do what Jeppe Hansen did. LOL*

Jeppe Hansen got fired from the Company for doing gay porn. Now he has a mansion in California—according to Snapchat.

Would you do it? Nathan types.

You should be the one in ballet school

Except I know he wouldn't last a week. Nathan's the biggest slacker there is, because his parents are so strict with him. I never see that side of them though. Whenever I'm at Nathan's place, they keep us supplied with a steady stream of delivery pizza and canned soda, and tell me to call them John and Stella because they want me to feel at home. A couple of years ago, while my parents were still separated, I went camping with Nathan's family. It was mainly to avoid spending the holidays with Frank—he'd try to make me hang out with his girlfriend so that we'd "bond," when I already barely got to see him. Nathan spent most of that trip trying to stay away from direct sunlight and mosquitoes, while I went canoeing with John. Stella kept saying I was the son she never had, which was awkward, but luckily Nathan was hiding out in our tent and couldn't hear her.

I told him we should switch parents, that it would solve both our problems, and he said darkly, Be my guest.

From down the corridor, someone lets out a high-pitched yodel like a fire alarm, and is soon drowned out by whoops and shouts—the guys in the rec room, playing yet another Melee. The walls at the residence must have been made by the same people who build fake castles and plywood trees for the school's productions of *Swan Lake* or *The Sleeping Beauty*.

Say Hi to Stella and John for me

I wish I lived 2000 km from my parents

You've only got one more year

Then what?

Aren't you going to university?

You're not

Nathan's joined a new Facebook group called Aspiring Male Models International. He's been working his way through the member profiles, studying each one with the intense level of attention to detail that'll ensure his success in biomedical engineering (his fallback plan), if he has the sense to give up on this modelling kick he's been on for the last year or so. I suggested that he could specialize in a field like anti-aging research, and it seemed to pique his interest. A model's career is even shorter than a ballet dancer's.

Check this guy out, says Nathan. *Looks like a dancer*

I follow the link to his profile and click on the thumbnail. A very blond, very tan Tadzio clone poses in cuffed shorts and boat shoes, on the prow of a luxury yacht.

Nah. Calves too skinny. No muscle tone

Look who's talking, Nathan shoots back. Then he adds an emoji: a monkey with its hands over its mouth.

I want to add: *You should see me now.* I don't, because that would only encourage him. Now that I'm dancing five hours a day, six days a week, I've gained muscles I didn't know existed. Still, I can't compete with the Tadzios of the online world. Aside from his over-processed hair and emerald-green contacts, he probably used Photoshop or a face filter at least.

I'm gonna DM him, Nathan says.

I send friend requests to a sociology major at Harvard and a Berlin filmmaker who's into thrash metal. One day I'll travel the world, and it'll be good to know people with couches to crash on. Unless I make it into the Aspirant

Program where you get to tour with the Company (though you still have to share hotel rooms).

I'm an only child, so I never had to share a room till last September, except for when Nathan and I had sleepovers. We stopped in Grade Nine because people thought it was weird when all of Nathan's other friends were girls. I've since realized it's weirder being surrounded by people you've got nothing in common with except ballet.

After I've graduated and joined the company, and after I get my big break—like stepping into a leading role when a principal gets injured, then getting transferred to the National Ballet of Canada—I'll buy a penthouse on Lakeshore. And if we're both still single, I'll ask Nathan to be my roommate. We'll be old by then, twenty-five maybe.

Nathan says I should dream on. That I'll probably end up stuck in Winnipeg, snowed in for good. I don't tell him it feels more like I'm floating out to sea on an ice shelf that broke off a glacier. The longer I'm here, the farther away home seems. Winter won't last forever. The world will thaw and I'll land somewhere else, eventually.

Sometimes, I try to imagine what life was like before the Internet. You could run away, change your name, and none of your new friends would know your true identity. Perhaps you wouldn't know either, after a while. Your past life would start to feel unreal. Like scrolling through photos on a stranger's phone.

In a Facebook group called Friends of Classical Ballet, I find a woman in Nevada who makes horse sculptures on her ranch. There are real horses in her photos.

Good evening Miss, I'm a Grade 12 student at the Royal Winnipeg Ballet School. It's minus forty and winter hasn't officially started yet. Nevada looks nice.

All I wanted from my parents was for them to tell me right from wrong. It would be so much easier than having to try everything IRL. Like making new friends, when everyone seems to be hiding behind a fairy-tale facade as unconvincing as the storyline of most ballets. Nevada's probably more like a desert outback full of rattlesnakes and hit men in hiding. But how will I know for sure?

Hey Nathan, wanna drive to Nevada?
How will you get out of Winterpeg?
I mean next summer
Mom signed me up to volunteer in Africa

I want to ask Stella to sign me up too. To tell me that I should volunteer because it builds character and you'll make friends for life—or at least learn how to hang on to the ones you have.

You have strength of character, Ms. Dianova said, and that's the most important ingredient.

If I wasn't so out of breath from all those *fouettés* she makes me do (twenty-four on my right leg, thirty-two on the left, my weak leg), I'd have asked her what she meant. Important like a once-in-a-lifetime chance, or like the air we can't live without breathing?

Whatever it was, she's given me hope. Maybe in time I'll figure out what the second and third most important ingredients are. I know something's missing. Something I can only sense by its absence, potent as a pinch of salt.

MARRIAGE

Perhaps it was my fault that Frank ended up in Ollie's room, on the single bed that someone had passed down to us while I was pregnant, for when baby outgrew his crib. That year, friends and relatives had showered us with hand-me-downs like consolation prizes. Frank and I were officially engaged, and he'd managed to acquire a great-aunt's art nouveau ring. But we were waiting till he finished his thesis. I refused to give my parents the satisfaction of financing a shotgun wedding, partly because it would have meant showcasing my baby bump in a traditional, hip-hugging cheongsam.

But you look great in everything, said Frank, unhelpfully.

Don't you think it would be just a bit ironic?

Wouldn't it be ironic…, Frank warbled in a mock-operatic falsetto.

When I didn't laugh, he said: Aren't you impressed by my conditional tense?

The Alanis Morissette hit had been a singalong favourite at the drunken end of undergrad kitchen parties.

I wanted to argue that having a family before marriage was against my parents' values, even if it wasn't planned—so wasn't it a bit late for compromise? But there was no need. Frank's never questioned my choices, though sometimes I wish he had.

Ollie's bed lay untouched, the covers dusty and unwrinkled for three years, till Frank suggested it was time to start the transition and move the crib out of our room. I didn't see the point. Ollie spent most nights asleep in the crook of my arm, with Frank rolled away from us, face to the wall. But I

had to admit that the crib could barely contain our growing
beanstalk.

Alone in his new room across the hall, Ollie fussed each
night till I got out of bed and fetched him back. Minutes
later, Frank would carry our sleeping son out again. I'd wake
an hour later to hear faint mewling. This dance went on for
years. One sleepless night, Frank picked up his pillow and
shuffled toward the door.

Where are you going? I whispered over Ollie's head.

In the doorway, Frank turned to face me. The light from
the hallway couldn't hide the darkness under his eyes.

They're not going to extend my TA fellowship again if I
don't finish this year, he said, and closed the door behind him.
Footsteps, then the sound of Ollie's door opening and closing.

My child slept on at my breast, still half-latched. I prised
him off gently and wiped the snail's trail of milky dribble
from lips and nipple. The bed seemed bigger, less cozy. Was
that how Ollie felt when left alone in his room? He was six
years old. How much longer before he got used to it?

We became homeowners the following year, thanks to a small
inheritance from Frank's grandmother. It was a year of naive
optimism, in retrospect, the year Frank finally completed
his PhD and won a research assistant job almost identical
to the one he'd had as a student, except that the salary was
slightly smaller.

In the new house, Ollie seemed to forget that he had
ever been afraid of sleeping alone. I stopped wearing my
blouses permanently unbuttoned; milk-stained because I'd
long foregone nursing bras. Frank and I finally tied the knot,
and Ollie agreed to squeeze into his Lord Fauntleroy suit

for the ceremony, on condition that he don a ball gown for the reception.

We were posing for wedding photos on the front steps of Old City Hall when my father joked that with all his costume changes, Ollie made the perfect traditional Chinese bride. I'm the only one in that photo who isn't laughing. Frank said that I must have been dreaming about the Peking Duck on the menu for that evening's banquet. But a ripple of doubt had stiffened my spine and turned the mild October afternoon suddenly chilly.

Goofing around on the stone steps with my best friend and maid of honour's son Nathan, Ollie looked carefree and dishevelled—like every other seven-year-old. When the boys grew tired of wrestling each other, they straddled the iron handrail and slid down, shrieking like schoolgirls.

What did they get up to on those sleepovers?

Come back here, Nathan! yelled Stella. You too, Ollie— you're going to split your pants!

Don't worry about the pants, I called out. Ollie will be thrilled to get rid of them.

I don't know how you manage to stay so cool, said Stella, and bent to rearrange the fishtail train of my vintage forties lace-and-rayon dress. You're like the anti-Bridezilla.

I thanked her silently. Marriage would not turn me into my mother, who had smiled at my father's joke earlier with uncharacteristic indulgence.

Just weeks ago, Ollie had returned from Nathan's house and announced that he wanted a Barbie doll too. It was all I could do to stop myself from asking what he thought other kids at school might think of him, teachers as well.

The photographer was herding us into place for another group shot, shouting cues presumably meant to relax us:

What's your favourite romantic comedy? Tell us a funny line. You're allowed to kiss—you're married now!

Behind him, a small group of tourists had gathered, and the Queen streetcar rumbled past. I placed one hand around my husband's waist, the other on my son's shoulder. I promised myself that no matter what, he'd always be my Oliver, my everything, my perfect boy.

I recall Frank's face, ruddy and unlined before the wedding, fading through Ollie's prepubescent years, till my husband all but disappeared—to take up residence in his TA's co-op, three blocks away from our double-mortgaged, Riverdale semi-detached.

Maybe old family photos have replaced actual memories, but it's the old Frank that comes to mind most readily. The face I still expect to find when I go downstairs, barefoot in the dark, on my way to fetch a drink of water after yet another trip to the bathroom. My toes feel for the edge of each tread, my hand on the banister, not trusting my eyes till I reach the bottom and see the light seeping out from under the kitchen door.

I know it's not Ollie—he's in bed by eleven most nights and up at dawn, to squeeze in ballet practice before school. Still, I'm startled by this vision of the father of my son: a greying, near-middle-aged academic, alone in the kitchen at three a.m.

What's the matter, Rose? Frank glances up from his laptop at the sight of me, glasses smudged, bathrobe askew.

What are you reading? He could be returning emails, trading stocks, or cruising BDSM dating sites for all I know. I slap the thought away. You seem upset, he says. Want some brandy?

Beside the window, the water purifier drips with disheartening regularity into a chipped saucer.

Sounds as good an idea as any, I say.

We sit across from each other, my husband and I, drinking out of necessity. Frank's eyes flicker as he reads, emitting snorts of laughter every few minutes. We never did share the same sense of humour. There were other things—weren't there?

I'm worried about Ollie, I say.

He nods. What's new?

The question sounds unforgivably callous.

If you have to ask, I begin, then change my mind.

At least Frank's back. For which we are all thankful. Though living a stone's throw away for three years, in a hippie commune, with a girl whose facial piercings apparently outnumbered her tattoos, shouldn't have prevented him from participating in his son's life if he'd wanted to. I used to run into him at The Big Carrot in the prepared meals section, or spot him from afar on his way to the subway station—head down, hunched under the weight of books in his backpack, as if our student days had never ended. For the first year of our unofficial separation, my first impulse was to roll down the window of our '98 Honda Civic and ask if he needed a ride. It took all the willpower I could muster to detour in the opposite direction, steered by my mother's conviction that it was best for Ollie, cross-legged in the back seat, engrossed in a well-thumbed copy of *International Figure Skating Magazine* (the one with Patrick Chan on the cover), to be protected from unplanned sightings of his missing father.

I run through a mental list: things about Ollie that we've previously discussed but failed to (re)solve (should we allow him to go backpacking with Nathan in Europe this summer, or mandate the chess and math camp my parents have offered to pay for?); things about Ollie that Frank may be unaware of or is doing a damn fine job of ignoring (does he realize that Ollie still sleeps with his favourite stuffed toy, the one Stella gave him for his tenth birthday, against my objections?); things I could be imagining entirely (despite all attempts to short-circuit the gnawing worries that lead to lurid visualization).

And now this relatively recent obsession with ballet (what was wrong with the at least borderline-normal hobbies of jazz, tap, ballroom and skating?), which has escalated into the outrageous idea of moving to a remote province, in a different time zone, to attend a boarding school for would-be professional ballet dancers. He's only one year away from finishing high school, for God's sake. Can't he at least wait till university to *grand jeté* his way out of the nest?

I dread to think what dorm life with a herd of hormonally imbalanced, body-conscious teenagers is going to do to his grades. Thank goodness my parents convinced me to fast-track Ollie through the sciences. I bribed him by saying it would leave him free to pursue things he really enjoyed, whatever they might be. Who knew he'd take me at my word?

I say: Stella still thinks that Ollie and Nate, you know …

Frank looks up, and he has the temerity to seem surprised. Of course—he wasn't around at the time. To him, the incident in question is about as real as a piece of high school required reading; CanLit skimmed in between smoking your first joint and losing your virginity. Though two years after the fact, my knee-jerk suspicions seem just as unreal. The palpable but groundless fear that when Ollie and Nate were discovered naked in Stella's new infrared sauna, they were exhibiting more than a universal male propensity for communal bathing and spas (even Frank goes *au naturel* in

the gym locker room). Curiosity is natural. Adolescence can
at times resemble a science experiment.

These days I'm kept awake by a deeper dread, no less irra-
tional: that I'll learn that Ollie has indeed been deflowered
by, say, the captain of the cheerleading squad.

Who cares what Stella thinks? says Frank. It's just a dis-
traction from her own life. He interlaces his fingers behind
his head and rocks back on the wooden chair. The chair legs
squeak on the ceramic tile.

I have to admit it's comforting, this uncommon smugness
we both relish now that *our* worst, it seems, has passed.

Doesn't stop her from taking it out on me, I say.

Then cut her off.

I reach for the bowl of unsalted almonds that's been sitting out for days now, going stale.

I'm not like you, I say. I just wonder sometimes, well, what
makes her think she's right?

Right about her son being in the closet, or that Ollie is too?

Frank! My hand goes to my mouth in spite of myself.
He's your *son*.

Rosie ... He removes his thick-rimmed glasses carefully,
with both hands. (I wonder if he pulls this move in the classroom too, this deliberate unmasking, revealing the depth
and intensity of his eyes.) It's not that I don't care, he says,
but God knows what we got up to at his age.

And I suppose you think we turned out all right.

Yes, says Frank. I do.

We're not drunk, I think. When was the last time we got
drunk? Truly, madly, deeply, I-can't-remember-your-name
drunk.

In the weeks following Frank's departure, I contemplated
getting a tattoo. I trawled the Internet for inspiration and

doodled designs, avoiding anything remotely suggestive of yin-yang or peace symbols. Once I started looking, it seemed that body art was everywhere, predictable as a mid-life crisis. Meanwhile, I continued to deflect the recommendations of well-meaning hairstylists, refusing to experiment with colour despite encroaching grey. In the end, I settled for piercing my ears—something I'd wished for as a child. I started with a pair of minimalist, geometric silver studs that, to my surprise and disappointment, my mother actually approved of.

Was she softening with age? Would time erode our differences, grain by grain, till I forgot the things I'd spent my life resisting?

Be patient, she said, above the chorus of my feminist friends advocating divorce and online dating. He'll come back. He'll realize he was wrong.

I clung to this prediction like a mantra, as if its repetition could make it true.

So far, it seems, this time my mother was right.

Last June, Frank walked in through the back door. He dumped his knapsack on the mudroom floor and headed for the living room where Ollie was doing his homework. I was in the kitchen and dropped everything but the bread knife to run toward the sound of an unseen intruder. In the doorway, I skidded to a halt.

Frank held both hands up in the air and said: I rang the buzzer.

His sudden reappearance wasn't really all that sudden. We'd been exchanging emails and phone calls for more than a year, discussing the implications of recommitment. He'd agreed to sleep in the basement, while we continued to hash things out. At some point, we started sharing a bed again. By then, Frank had replaced the doorbell's long-dead battery.

This late-night encounter, over brandy and stale nuts, is typical of our usual patterns of communication. Cagey and inconclusive, with no apparent urgency. My indecision and self-doubt. Frank's laconic responses. The problem is, we're discussing Ollie's future, not ours.

It's just not like him, I say. For something like that to go on for years, without him telling us ... My eyes brim with selfish tears.

To his credit, Frank stays silent, not asking for clarification I can't provide.

What do you think? I say finally. Should we let him go?

Frank snorts. And when was the last time Master Oliver sought our permission, let alone our advice?

But we're *paying* for it, I say helplessly. It's only half true: Ollie's been offered a full scholarship. Our main contribution will be the return-trip airfare.

Frank gazes steadily at me. I recognize the same mixture of absorption and distractedness that I've seen in Ollie when he's tackling a new skill or challenge.

Go on, I think. Tell me what I'm thinking, tell me what I'm feeling.

He reaches for his glasses and says, I don't know.

The old longing rears up in me; the umbilical cord drawn taut before being cut forever. If I took off my bathrobe now, would Frank pull me up onto the kitchen table and mount me? Like the first and last time we attempted to re-enact that scene from *The Postman Always Rings Twice*, in our student apartment? I still remember the laminate countertop, cold as a slab of marble. Our perseverance was inextinguishable. Twenty years later, my spontaneity wavers. My mind previews a farce: the bathrobe half-on, half-off, its belt wedged beneath me as we mount the table, trying to avoid Frank's laptop; me struggling to keep a section of terry cloth under my thighs to protect the cherry wood tabletop.

At least it's ballet, I say, and not, I don't know, dancing in a male strip club or something.

There you go, says Frank, and turns back to his computer.

Is he intentionally withholding the comfort of his laughter, grainy and well-worn as a dog-eared snapshot tucked in a wallet? Perhaps he's simply decided that stoic acceptance is the best policy.

By Grade Five, Ollie's self-produced pageants had been replaced by gymnastics routines. I was amazed by how quickly his precocious flexibility and sense of balance translated into a flair for figure skating. Lots of boys skate—there's hockey, isn't there? He'd show up early to his lessons and practise by the boards. I'd point him out to other parents: That's my son, Oliver. The look on their faces when he landed his double axel. By the time he asked for ballet lessons, he'd mastered every other dance style and won the leading role in the school production of *Grease*, even though his voice had only just broken and he was, at age thirteen, about a foot shorter than the leading girl.

The Royal Winnipeg Ballet School takes only a handful of male students each year. Why should it matter that it's not a path I've chosen for him?

I've been cradling my near-empty glass for so long, the last trickle of brandy is the same temperature as my blood. When I swallow, my throat catches fire and I remember my thirst, the reason I'm here when I should be upstairs, fast asleep, whether or not my husband's beside me.

Frank's head is drooping now, his breaths rhythmic and harsh, his glasses slipped to the end of his nose. I steady one hand on the table and suck in my stomach, so I can wiggle out of my chair without scraping it back against the floor. The icy tiles repel my bare feet, and I tiptoe to the water purifier with none of Ollie's grace.

Where does he get it from? Who made this child, so separate from his pedestrian parents? The boy turned pied piper, dancing toward the future while we lag behind: ill-prepared homebodies, thrust into the continuing education of learning to be a couple again.

Is it too soon to tell Frank about that MFA in Creative Writing I've had my eye on ever since Stella told me she started a wine-tasting course and is working toward her Diploma in Culinary Arts?

Will Ollie's love for ballet last?

What'll he do twenty years from now, when he's worn down by the inevitable injuries of this physically gruelling art?

Note to self: next time I'm at the computer, look up the health insurance plan provided by the school; if inadequate, purchase more comprehensive coverage.

And while I'm online, take a closer look at the UBC syllabus. I already know the faculty includes one of my favourite poets—my heart did a *petit sauté* when I spotted his back cover photograph—that soul patch, that beatnik cool.

Frank stirs in his sleep and his arm slides across the table, toward his empty glass. Instinctively I scoop it up, ready to pop it in the dishwasher—but that would mean another barefoot trek across the tiles, so I set it back on the table.

Outside the kitchen, I pause at the foot of the stairs, my hand on the dimmer switch. The honeyed half-light catches the top of Frank's head where smooth, pale skin gleams beneath thinning hair in the spot he scrupulously hides with longer top layers that fade into shorter, silvered sides.

I'll keep the light on. That way, if he wakes before dawn, he'll be spared the shock of disorientation upon waking alone in the dark—that blind, breathless moment before you realize you've been here all along.

Setting Fire to Water

T he end came faster than he could have hoped. Copernicus, twenty-nine, balding since seventeen, who could be seen each morning at his company's office building through the tinted windows of the fourth-floor gym, a ghost with fluorescent aura being slowly erased by encroaching daybreak; who hadn't taken a vacation since joining this above-average, but only just, medium-to-large corporation of chartered accountants (specializing in US taxation and non-Canadian residents) as an intern fresh out of York University; who'd finally proposed to the stylish and almost always confident Emmeline from *Excellence!* magazine (floors six and seven) after a rocky three years of on-again, off-again courtship—punctuated sometimes by diffidence on Copernicus's part, more often by the lady's penchant for explosive affairs with tousled, taciturn guitarists invariably California-bound—had conclusively determined once and for all, six weeks post popping the question, that this engagement was as stalled as an out-of-service elevator, ever since Emmeline claimed to have lost her Birks princess cut solitaire at the indoor pool, only for it to resurface a week later in the ground-floor recycling room.

All Copernicus could think, on opening his office door to the zealous, newly hired cleaner who answered his LOST notice in the VIP lounge, was that traces of his own recent yet utterly foreign youth were painfully reproduced in this boy's hopeful, African-American visage. At least Copernicus had the presence of mind to tip him a fifty-dollar bill (was the reward too small or too large?).

Copernicus—"Nic" to his peers and superiors, "Sir" to the clueless and recently recruited—who'd twice been named Young Accountant of the Year (2008 and 2010) by the Institute for the Personal Growth and Enrichment of Chartered Professional Accountants, and was halfway through the eighty-hour Certification in Advanced First Aid (complimentary for employees keen to upgrade the basic requirements of workplace health and safety, which seemed rather, well, *basic*), suddenly found himself divested of the townhouse he'd acquired mere months ago in hopes of matrimony—"It's a seller's market," his realtor assured him, "Not so good for the buyer, but leave town for long enough and the wind will change"—his wardrobe condensed to a couple of Ralph Lauren polo shirts and Banana Republic chinos in an Eddie Bauer duffel bag, his request to resign countered by a paid sabbatical (reluctantly accepted), and an open-return airline ticket to India tucked between passport pages in the interior compartment of his fanny pack.

The fanny pack was a relic from his first and last trip abroad, aged eighteen, on a European tour bus. As soon as he buckled it round his waist, he remembered shuffling through the streets of Paris, a disposable raincoat pulled over his protuberant cargo, embarrassment outweighing the thing's multi-zippered convenience. So, that gut-clenching discomfort hadn't just been the last vestiges of adolescent angst compounded by too much borscht, eventually purged in a Bucharest hostel bathroom.

Perhaps it was a bad omen. Better find some other repository for his essentials. But the taxi was already at his front door.

And now, as if to underscore a point, he could feel the black leather belt bag gouging a fist-sized cavity in the soft flesh of his lower abdomen, uncomfortably close to the pubic bone, as he strained over the edge of a small motorboat somewhere along the River Ganges, a box of matches in one hand and an unlit tea-light in the other.

Less than an hour ago, one hundred rupees had bought him the white candles in pleated paper cups, each one garlanded with withered marigolds in a banana-leaf boat. He hadn't wished for thirteen of them but the street vendor snatched his vaguely proffered bank bill, leaving Copernicus with the familiar sensation of having gained more than he'd bargained for—except there had been no bargaining.

"You have no initiative, Nicky," Emmeline had said. "It was my idea to get engaged."

"But I arranged for the photographer and the bandoneon."

"You know I don't like French music."

"It wasn't French," he began. "Just because we were in Montreal that weekend—"

"Forget it," she sighed. "Why don't you try using your imagination?"

She was dissatisfied. This Copernicus could see with increasing clarity as he pounded the treadmill, watched his reflection in the floor-to-ceiling windows disappear and, in the week of the engagement ring's absence, as he carefully sifted through the contents of every vacuum cleaner in the building. After the ring was returned, he couldn't recall if she'd actually put it back on.

Now the sun was rising above the Ganges, a rose-gold orb grazing the far shore. On the opposite side, a crescent moon floated above a crumbling palace, an open-air crematorium, and men and women bathing in the thick green waters. Submerged to their waists, still clothed in their undergarments, the bathers seemed oblivious to the proximity of corpses laid on the shore beneath colourful, patterned shrouds. Copernicus had seen similar designs on bed sheets and tablecloths hanging from washing lines and among market wares on his ride from airport to hotel, bouncing in the back of a tuk-tuk, blasted by exhaust fumes and the inescapable stench of burning waste that seemed to permeate the whole country—paper, plastics, cow dung, human flesh.

The bathers laughed and jostled as they cupped water in their hands and poured it over each other—the same water anointed the living and the dead. Daily, the bathers prepared for their own funerals, joyfully awaiting their turns to be consumed by fire.

Copernicus had joined an excursion of Americans, his passage bought with his offering of candles. "For the river god," Copernicus told them cheerfully. He couldn't remember exactly what he'd read as he surfed the net, inputting search phrases such as "backpacking to seek meaning of life" or "atheist spiritual quest India?"

"Simply divine," gushed one lady, burying her nose in the marigolds.

Copernicus thought of the hawker's blackened fingers.

"So you're Canadian, eh?" said her husband.

"Sorry?" Copernicus wondered if the giveaway was his accent or the Roots logo on his baseball cap.

"I've been to Toronto," the husband went on with unnerving clairvoyance. "I went up the CN Tower and I swear I could see Rochester, but you can't get a good picture from behind glass."

According to the Personal Income Questionnaire routinely given to all clients, you pay taxes according to where you made money in the last twelve months. Further questioning of the past is irrelevant. You fill in the form to the best of your knowledge and leave the rest to the feds. You spend your life wading through similar forms, inputting data against the clock. For the whole of his adult life, Copernicus and the clock had been cruising neck and neck in a race whose outcome was fixed. Still, he enjoyed a certain unquantifiable and vicarious thrill: the sense that something of his opponent's tireless resilience and, well, *immortality*, was being transferred to him by virtue of sheer exposure—much like the double-edged effects of UV rays. In rare, superhuman moments Copernicus even took the lead, never for long but just enough to earn accolades like most-promising, second-in-line, probable husband-to-be of the evasive Emmeline, who had recently been appointed Beauty Editor and was poised to ascend the Everest of *Excellence!* via Art Director to, one day, Editor-in-Chief.

Copernicus struck the first match. You make a wish, cast the candles to the river, and watch them flicker, fire on water—or so he'd read online.

The match went out. None of the websites had warned him about the wind.

Copernicus struck another match and sheltered the feeble flame with his hand. It took to the wick for a few breathless seconds—"Ooh," gasped his fellow passengers—then fizzled out.

In the green water, banana-leaf boats drifted by. In the boats were spent candles, oozing and misshapen with short, blackened wicks. Most of the marigold garlands were incomplete or missing altogether.

Copernicus shook the matchbox and it rattled like a broken toy. Some of the matches landed in his hand; others fell onto the deck and lay intermingled with those already spent.

"Hang in there, folks," said Copernicus. "Too early to give up yet."

His voice was not his own. It was the voice of breakfast television, of inconsequential reports on food and fashion, and interviews with minor celebrities. The voice whiled away the grey, pre-dawn hours, occasionally interrupted by more serious segments on world news and weather. It twittered on in the background in the cardio corner, muffled by the treadmill's motor, comforting as a dawn chorus. Except on TV there was always laughter, even if it was canned.

The expressions on this audience's faces were blank, a puzzle. The boatman gazed with implausible fascination at the sky. Probably he didn't understand English.

The websites called India "the spiritual centre of the world," as if India was not a country but an essential, hidden organ without which no other country could exist. A purplish, pulpy spleen or belaboured heart, distended and riddled with veins. The world flocked to India to discharge its ills and be recharged by life-giving forces not found in the staple North American diet: the zeal of devotion, the taxation of ritual, the rapture of sacrifice. Surfing the web late into the night, Copernicus pieced together a vision of a hitherto unimaginable way of life; a life which, if it had previously, incongruously been presented to him among the glossy pages of the *Condé Nast Traveler*, would have horrified him. He would perform the rites of penance till his hair grew past his shoulders. He would backpack through the desert till his sandals were shreds. He would learn to live without money.

He would sleep naked under a sky where the sun and moon coexisted peacefully, as in ancient times when there was no such thing as death.

Copernicus himself would vanish, leaving no trace except perhaps the memory of love—self-conscious, precarious, and half-baked, but love nonetheless.

By now, the stack of spent matches at Copernicus's feet resembled a miniature pyre. He crushed the empty matchbox and dropped it on the heap.

"Um ... does anyone have a lighter?"

The propeller churned. The audience was slow to react. There was a rustling of windbreakers, of crackling static as they groped in their pockets, fumbled among bottles of mineral water, sunblock, Advil, granola bars, mosquito repellent. Between them, they were well-prepared for a multitude of small calamities. It occurred to Copernicus that these people could not imagine other, more critical emergencies involving the need to swim, or failing to swim, or sinking like a stone in the opaque water.

Take the craft that bore them, a vessel doomed to fail a safety inspection at any respectable marina back home. Where were the lifejackets, the distress flares, the spare drain plugs? Copernicus glanced around for the capacity plate— wasn't the boat listing toward starboard on account of one passenger whose girth was the equal of two? As for his own uncharacteristic indifference—shouldn't he be feeling more alarmed, or curious at least?

There had been one morning, unprepossessing as all the others at first, when Copernicus had accelerated the speed of his treadmill, by increments, toward the speed of light. His finger depressed the keypad's up arrow, haltingly at first, then unremittingly as the digital display climbed, till his feet seemed to glide, near effortless, above the spinning belt. Copernicus spread his arms in the gesture of a marathoner at the finish line, primed for flight, ready to burst through that hazy threshold between dreamer and dream. At the moment of crossing, the machine betrayed his trust. His next step skewed inward, his ankle torqued, a shooting pain flung him off course into the handrail. The machine kept running. A fellow early bird hurried over with a timid "Are you all right?"—as if "all right" was any plausible description for this tumble out of sublime weightlessness into winded mortality. Copernicus stayed motionless, head bowed, gripping the handrail, his breaths harsh and irregular, above the indifferent purr of looping black rubber. The Samaritan retreated.

His ankle had sustained a light swelling, not even a bruise. Still, he reduced his cardio routine to the elliptical trainer and rowing machine, while the full spectrum of the humanly possible continued to shimmer each dawn, reflected in those lightly tinted windows: the tireless, ghostly runners. There was no obstacle to transcendence except your own lack of faith.

As he watched the Americans rummage through their drugstore supplies, seeking some sort of fire-starting device and finding none, Copernicus felt the stirrings of a reluctant foreboding. Without intending to, he found himself searching his own pockets even though he had smoked less than a handful of cigarettes in his life, all of them in some poorly lit bar after an inadvisable amount of alcohol, in the aching, ever-restless company of Emmeline, whose presence was at this moment more palpable than when she was within reach.

He found the bullet-sized bit of black plastic—a logo, "Neo World," inscribed in silver on one side—in the secret compartment of his fanny pack. You depress a switch at its centre and a USB jack pops out from one end of the bullet. It had taken Copernicus a month after receiving this cryptic gift from his betrothed (though it was December, it wasn't a stocking stuffer, and his birthday was two months away) to figure out that when the switch was pushed in the opposite direction, a coiled tungsten filament was activated, brightening within seconds to a glowing amber.

He stowed this token of Emmeline's affections—those gossamer-fine, insubstantial traces of warmth and promise, impossible to grasp without resorting to representation in grosser terms (a 0.59 carat diamond, tickets to the opera, a whiff of Chanel Cristalle, a hybrid USB flash drive and flameless lighter)—in the breast pocket of his suit jacket. Often, he forgot it was there and turned it in to the dry cleaners' along with the suit. This was of no consequence since he never put Neo World to either of its intended uses. While packing for the pilgrimage he had slipped it into his fanny pack as an afterthought, unsure of what it signified anymore (if anything at all). Emmeline might as well have given him a vial of her blood. It occurred to Copernicus that such a gift would be as meaningless as the object currently in his palm.

Copernicus's fellow passengers sat on the gunwales, their upturned faces as baffled as the wilted marigolds with their moulting, wind-ruffled petals. The banana-leaf boats were clustered on top of the wooden box that housed the motor. They trembled and shook along with the warped, splitting boards covered with peeling blue paint.

"Throw *him* to the river god," came an anonymous jest, a stage whisper. A few halting guffaws followed in uneasy tandem, lost to the wide river and boundless skies.

"You know," said Copernicus to his audience, "An unlit candle is the greater sacrifice. An invisible flame will never die."

No one laughed. A strange spark had been struck by the edge in his voice, a blade newly unsheathed, forged in fire, quenched in brine. Copernicus had no time to wonder where it came from, this sudden flare that had passed through him like an electric current, whose only evidence was the briefest of flames that had flickered blue against blue skies—*was it really there?*—then vanished. Already its heat was fading.

Copernicus held up Neo World like a magician's hand—*now you see it, now you don't*—and released it to the water with a flick of his wrist. "Get it?"

The silver typeface caught the morning sunlight and flashed once before the lighter sank beneath the surface. Above, seagulls swerved and circled. They flapped their wings briefly then let the air currents carry them, surfing as long as they could without falling from the sky. Big-bellied, overfed by tourists, they had no reason to fly.

"Hurry," said Copernicus, "or we'll be back on shore and you wouldn't want bad luck now, would you?"

Grumbling, they obeyed. There were eight or nine of them and they were middle-aged or older, and less than agile. They assembled in a loose train and took turns tottering the few swaying steps between motor and gunwale. Kneeling on the damp, splintered wooden ledge and bending over the railing—cautiously lowering their offerings to the water and releasing them at the last possible moment—was not easy. They did so anyway, with care, as if their candles were lit, as if solemnity would imbue their actions with portentousness.

As if, for the first time in his life, Copernicus was the only person not taking himself seriously.

He perched on the edge of the prow and wondered if he ought to apologize, to call out, "Wait, I didn't mean this, it was a mistake," or if their actions had nothing to do with him, just as the Copernicus who had spoken to them moments before was the shadow of someone he'd never imagined the existence of—an existence he already doubted.

In the end, he said nothing. They had wordlessly devised this unorthodox ritual all by themselves. Their faith was sudden and inexplicable.

Afterwards they slumped on the gunwales near the stern. They cast meek, furtive glances at him and muttered among themselves.

"I think we've been scammed."

"Made us look like fools."

"Might be one of the locals—looks can be deceiving."

"But he didn't want money."

Their voices drifted like the gulls.

Copernicus leaned forward on the prow, suddenly exhausted. He watched a man squatting in the shallows by the fast-approaching shoreline. Ankle-deep in muddy water, the man appeared to cradle some small object in his hands, rinsing and turning it, dipping it beneath the water's surface, lifting it up again so sand and water poured through. Copernicus tried to make out what the man handled with such reverence, but always something else—a gull diving for a piece of thrown bait, another boatload of tourists— obscured the picture.

Copernicus watched, mesmerized, as the man lifted up his long white robes and tucked them neatly between his loins before wading in deeper. Now he bent closer toward the water, submerged his arms up to the elbows, moved them gently back and forth. Stray pieces of garbage floated past and brushed his skin. Perhaps he was searching for some tiny object accidentally displaced in the process of cleansing; a lost fragment of no significance to anyone else.

The smell of burning waste that hung over the city had extended across the river, refusing to be dispersed by the wind. Now, as they neared the harbour, its pungency seemed to intensify and Copernicus recognized the acrid aroma of gasoline. At the same time he heard a soft, slurping sound as the ridged soles of his all-terrain sandals squelched against the wooden deck. The boards beneath his feet were slick with a liquid more viscous than water, iridescent and rainbowed.

The boatman was standing on the stern behind his passengers, arms folded, steering with his foot. Had he known all along that the engine was leaking?

The gasoline had seeped out from a corner of the blue box and soaked through the used matches littering the deck. Each match was wasted tinder, a missed opportunity, having failed to fulfil the basic function without which it had no reason to exist: to bring fire to this sluggish, dispirited world.

Copernicus bent and picked up one of the matches with his index finger and thumb, brought it to his nostrils and sniffed it. Out of the corner of his eye, he saw the other passengers regarding him with contempt.

He sprang to his feet and half-fell against the railing, but did not reach for it; his hands were too busy pulling his pocket linings inside out, unzipping his windbreaker and divesting himself of it like a straitjacket, unbuckling his fanny pack, upturning and shaking it vigorously so that passport, ticket, and banknotes fluttered out. As if he might find among his depleted possessions one last ready-made tool for transcendence. As if he might discover a trick hidden up his own sleeve. As if Neo World, summoned by the force of his longing, would leap from the water like a flying fish to return to his hand.

Could a flameless lighter ignite liquid gasoline? Even if it had not been subjected to at least a dozen rounds of cleaning solvent and jet steam? Given the circumstances of a simpler world whose fantasies were still intact?

Copernicus recognized this voice, timid and questioning, a ghost on a turning wheel forever threatened with extinction by morning's light. He knew this ghost intimately, had grown so accustomed to its relentless commentary, whispered from the shadows of every scene from his short and stunted life, that he'd long assumed it was his own. Far more resonant now was that other voice whose first intimation had been a brief, scalding passage—of fire in the belly, of arcane orations—a voice that now leapt, uncontained, from stomach's pit to open mouth and echoed across the water, urgent as a siren: "Fire, fire!"

At once, a chorus of other voices threatened to drown him out.

"He's crazy!"

"Someone stop him, for God's sake."

For a moment Copernicus stalled, a thief caught in the act—did he dare claim this blazing voice?

The next moment a hand fell on his left shoulder and bore down; he shook it off in unthinking reflex. Another hand seized his right arm under the armpit. He brought his elbow to his face and turned bared teeth toward the fingers clutching his bicep; his incisors tore through air, molars gnashed, and he was released to duck out of reach. In one fleet step he mounted the gunwale's narrow ledge to stand teetering like a sail, both arms extended. Now he was staggering toward the tip of the prow, slipping and sliding down the wooden boards which narrowed toward a point without a railing. His rubber soles were frictionless as skates.

He had intended to turn back, to face the herd one last time with pride and defiance, to witness their terror as he

surpassed their earthbound imaginings. But his feet would
not adhere. His feet continued to glide forward, unstoppable.
The water was warmer than he'd expected. Copernicus sank
slowly through murky darkness. His feet had not reached the
riverbed before he rose again like a buoy and his head cleared
the surface. He choked and gasped for air, seeing nothing,
hearing only a confusion of shouts, bird cries, and the roar
of motorboats cruising, waiting for their turn to dock in the
congested harbour. Again he went under. The next time he
came up, he searched desperately for the promise of land but
the water was too crowded. He estimated the shore was about
twenty metres away.

A plastic wrapper floated into his mouth. He spat it out
with disgust, and simultaneously began to thrash and kick
furiously. Gradually, his body recalled the foreign motions of
long-forgotten, much-loathed swimming lessons. Spluttering
and half-blinded by the spray from his haphazard flailing, he
resurfaced and managed to keep his head more or less above
water, paddling like a dog.

A long time passed and Copernicus was still in the river. He
was beginning to tire and he swallowed water more often. The
wakes of passing boats battered and deluged him. Sometimes
he thought he glimpsed a figure in white robes crouched at the
river's edge but the vision remained in the distance, a blurred
speck. Perhaps he had only imagined it. Perhaps he had been
treading water all this time, or worse, swimming in circles.

A rope flew through the air and lashed Copernicus's back.
A passing fisherman prodded him with his oar. For a moment,
his ears became unclogged and he heard shouts of "Hello sir!
Over here!" and the sound of a boat's engine, very close.

Copernicus swam on, stubbornly, toward the last invisible
certainty. It could not be much farther.

Acknowledgements

Thank you to everyone who has supported the development of these stories. To Laure Baudot, Phil Dwyer, Jim Joyce, and Natalie Onuška, who critiqued numerous drafts. To John Burgess, Susan Glickman, and Seán Virgo, whose editorial wisdom and inspirations guided these stories through their final stages. I am especially indebted to Elizabeth Philips for her generous and insightful mentorship over the years.

This book has received support from the Ontario Arts Council, the Toronto Arts Council, and the Elizabeth Krehm Mentorship Award for Creative Writing from the Chang School at Ryerson University. A Professional Development Grant from Access Copyright Foundation enabled me to work on this book at the Sage Hill Fiction Colloquium.

"The Stain" began during a collaborative Oulipian exercise instigated by Corina Bardoff at Brooklyn Public Library.

Previous versions of some stories have appeared in print and online in the following publications:

"Model Shown Is Actual Size," *Still Point Arts Quarterly* (US, 2015)

"Parlour," *Asia Literary Review* (Hong Kong, 2014)

"Setting Fire to Water," *Litro Magazine* (UK, 2017)

"Setting Fire to Water," *On Fire* (Transmundane Press, US, 2017)

"The Real Macaron," 2020 Short Story Contest winner, *Equinox: Poetry and Prose* (US, 2021)

"The Truth About Aging," *High Shelf XXIX* (US, 2021)

"Words and Colour," *The Bombay Review* (US, India, 2020)

"Vintage Chanel and a Paper Fan," *The Humber Literary Review* (Canada, 2021)

Courtesy of Sullivan Hismans

Phoebe Tsang is a Hong-Kong born Chinese, British, and Canadian poet, author, librettist, and playwright. She has published a poetry collection, *Contents of a Mermaid's Purse* (Tightrope Books, 2009), and her short stories have appeared in *Geist, Broken Pencil Magazine, Litro Magazine, Rivet Journal, Asia Literary Review, The Bombay Review,* and other places. Her writing is informed by lyricism and rhythmic sense, inherited from her background as a professional classical violinist. *Setting Fire to Water* is her debut collection of stories.